FROM THE SENSES TO SENSUALITY

....

SIKEMAN

EMMI

EMMI Publications, LLC.
115 River Road
Ste. 112
Edgewater, NJ 07020

Publisher's Note: This is a work of fiction. Names, characters, places, and incidents are a product of the author's imagination. Locales and public names are sometimes used for atmospheric purposes. Any resemblance to actual people, living or dead, or to businesses, companies, events, institutions, or locales is completely coincidental.

Ordering Information:
Quantity sales. Special discounts are available on quantity purchases by corporations, associations, and others. For details, contact the "Special Sales Department" at the address above.

From the Senses to Sensuality/ Sikeman. -- 1st ed.
ISBN   978-0-9710672-2-6

This book is dedicated to all the women that I have known and who have provided me with their meanings and definitions of what sensuality is to them as women. Thank You and much love goes out to all of you.

She is the kind of woman that will drive you crazy by doing absolutely nothing except being herself.

–Daniel Saint

EMMI PUBLICATIONS

TABLE OF CONTENTS

1. The Party

2. The Fantasy Getaway

3. The Bet

4. The Kiss

5. Telephone Intimacy

6. Car Trouble

7. The Tigress

8. Dessert by Blindfold

9. Forbidden Fruit

10. The Scavenger Hunt

11. Old Love True Love

12. Threesome

PREFACE

Hey Ladies...

I have a surprise...
But first realize I must blindfold your mind's eye to set your
imagination free
I must tie up your inhibitions and release your passions
All it will take is a feather and a whisper.
The feather will caress your essence
The whisper will calm your tensions
My belief is that I can set your soul free
By just touching you without touching you
Loving you without making love to you
Stimulating you mentally, spiritually and emotionally
While physically treasuring your presence
But wait a minute...I want that feather to touch you in ways that have
never been imagined
I want every nerve ending in your body to pulsate and gyrate when the
feather embraces you.
I want an erotic fantasy to seem like reality when the right words are
whispered at the right time...
Now in the back of my mind I find myself wondering what else can I do
with a feather and a whisper?
It intrigues me to think that a feather and a whisper can entice me
more than a kiss...
There is no imagination in a kiss
But anything can come from a whisper

And a feather can become anything.

A whisper can be the perfect summer breeze on a sun-drenched afternoon.

A feather can be that fan that tickles your fancy with every stroke along the curves of your gorgeous womanly frames.

It's a shame that time doesn't allow me to name all of the things that a feather or a whisper can be.

But the truth is that only a few are needed to make you believe in the pure ecstasy of sensuality.

From the Senses to Sensuality

ONE

The Party

*E*dward knocked on the door nervously, not knowing what to expect once he crossed the threshold of the Velvet Palace. After thirty seconds, he knocked again. The door opened and standing in the doorway was a huge highly intimidating black bald security guard standing about 6'6" easily 330lbs, named Charles.

Edward walked through the door and Charles announced in a deep baritone voice,

"Welcome to the Velvet Palace...we are here to fulfill all of your erotic fantasies.

Now we do have some rules...the first and most important rule is...NO MEAN NO! Secondly, here is about mutual fulfillment, be aware of that."

As Edward walked in the corridor, there was a set of stairs. At the top of the stairs was a tall dark brown skinned woman. She was a large but portioned woman with very striking facial features and a smile that could light up the world.

"Welcome to the Velvet Palace, I am Lady Suave, your hostess. Here let me show you around." Edward apprehensively followed the hostess

Lady Suave asked,
"Is this your first time here?"

Edward slowly shook his head in the affirmative.

"Baby, its ok to speak, I won't hurt you, unless that is what you are into." And she let out a hardy laugh.

Edward nervously smiled and then giggled.

Lady Suave said,
"Baby, we are here to have fun. I know just what you need."

She took Edward by the hand and led him up a winding staircase. At the top of the stairs, there was a doorway with a black sheer veil across it. They walked through the veiled doorway and there sitting in a large plush black leather seat in the corner of the room sat this awe striking, stunningly beautiful light skinned woman sitting with her shapely legs crossed sipping on a drink and listening to Lalah Hathaway's One Mile. The music filled the room, but it wasn't overpowering. She was between twenty-eight and thirty years of age. She was about 5'5", weighing about 145 pounds and was stacked in all the right places. Her hair went to her mid back and was two toned, black and autumn brown. Her eyes were a deep mahogany brown and had a twinkle in them that just touched Edward's soul and she had two deep dimples in her cheeks when she smiled. You could tell she was of bi-racial origin.

Lady Suave said, "Nicole, this is someone who needs your services. I will leave you two to get acquainted."

Before Lady Suave exited the room, she turned Edward's hand over to Nicole as though she was relinquishing custody of him. Nicole sat her drink down on the stand that was right by her chair, stood up, gave Edward a quick glance over and said one word,

"Strip!"

Edward looked around as if to ask, "Are you talking to me?" but he never uttered a word. Edward looked at Nicole as he started unbuttoning his shirt. Slowly, one button at a time, not knowing what to say nor do, he *continued. Edward was admiring Nicole's beautiful face and body.*

She was wearing a gold and burgundy sheer silk sarong that wrapped around the curves of her well maintained athletic body. Edward could see her hardened nipples and was excited, but he did not show his excited state. At the third button Nicole said, "That's it baby, nice and slow. Put on a show for mama." and gave a devilish grin. After Edward had taken off his shirt, Nicole ran her slender index finger across his nipples and said,

"I bet you are ticklish?"

Edward smiled and said, "No, not really."

Nicole replied, "So you can speak, I thought I was dealing with a mute for a minute." and laughed.
Edward bashfully chuckled a little.
Then Nicole said, "OK, finish strippin' for mama."

Edward unbuttoned and unzipped his pant, but before he could take off his pant,
Nicole said, "Boxers or briefs?"

Edward looked down then looked up at Nicole and said,

"Commando."

Nicole proclaimed, "Alright now! We've got ourselves an undercover freak."

and gave that same devilish grin as before. After Edward was totally naked, Nicole instructed him to lie on the table face down. Nicole asked, "Are there any places on your body that has been injured or you don't want touched?" Edward answered, "No, I am fit as a fiddle and healthy as a horse." Nicole replied, in an almost Creole accent,

"Baaabee! I can see that and hung like one too!"

Nicole went over to her table of tricks and opened this basalt glass container. She poured the contents of the container onto Edward's back. The liquid was warm and soothing with a scent of lavender.

Nicole said, "I think you are gonna enjoy this...and if you don't...mama Nicole will."

Nicole let her sarong fall to the floor, revealing her beautiful naked body. She climbed onto Edward's back and began massaging his neck and shoulder areas.

"You are so tense, you are gonna make mama work this evening, Huh? Well don't worry, when mama is done with you, you are gonna be a new man."

She continued to work his upper body and used the rest of her body to apply the oil all over. She had a skill of application that could not be matched by anyone. She was the Mozart of massage. She really began to get into this unique body session. She began to use her feet and knees along with her hands, elbows and breasts to massage all along Edward's back, neck and shoulders. At one interval, she straddled his neck with her inner thighs and applied pressure. Edward let out a moan.

Nicole, said, "That feels good huh?"

Edward remained silent. Nicole continued,

"You just don't know how good this feels to me. I know I am getting deep into your muscles. I can feel them relax and release and that just turns me on!"

Nicole used her well-oiled shins to slide over Edward's buttocks and she felt the tension on the gluteus muscles. All of a sudden, she slapped him on his bare ass and said, "Relax baabee! Mama's got this...Oh I love a nice tight ass like this, gives mama something nice and hard to hold on too.
But you are not ready for all of that." Just then, the music changed. The song that began to play was, "Say yes", by Floetry. Nicole's mood changed from the free-spirited dominatrix to a shy little girl. She was almost melancholy. She stopped her massage, got off of

Edward's back and sat in her big leather chair. Edward
looked up at her and said,
  "Did I do something wrong?"
Nicole shook her head and answered, "No." quietly.
Edward noticed a tear rolling down Nicole's cheek. Upon
seeing this, Edward grabbed a towel off of the stand
where Nicole's massage oils were and wrapped it around
his waist. Edward walked over by Nicole's chair and sat
on the floor in front of her. Edward asked,
  "Are you sure everything is ok?"

Nicole answered, "Every time I hear this song, it makes

me think of my first love.... He died in a motorcycle

accident a few months back...I will be ok...just give me a

moment to compose myself..."

Edward responded empathically,
  "I know what it is like to lose someone you love...I
have been down that road...I recently lost someone that I
was close to myself...she died of cancer...I never told her
how I felt about her, but I really believe she knew...

I know we just met but, I am here for you if you just
want to talk or anything you need to help you feel
better..."

"Well thank you...you are so sweet..." Nicole replied as she bent forward and kissed Edward on his forehead.

At that point Edward noticed how beautifully Nicole's nails were polished. Edward asked,
   "Do you do your own toes?"
Nicole looked at her toes then looked at Edward, smiled and said,
   "You know, no man has ever asked me that...I get myself a mani-pedi whenever I can."
   Edward asked, "Can I caress your feet?"

Nicole replied, "That is two for two, no man has ever

asked me that either. Yes, you can."

Edward began to rub Nicole's feet handling them gently but with a firm grip. Nicole just relaxed back in her big plush leather chair. Edward stated,
   "You are the one who needs the massage..." Then Edward paid close attention to how Nicole reacted with the different motions and techniques he used while massaging her feet and calves. Nicole sat back and said nothing. She picked up her drink with one hand and wiped the tear away with the other.
   As the music continued to play, Nicole got more and more relaxed, listening to the refrain of the song, "All you gotta do is say yes, don't deny whatcha feel let me

undress you baby, open up your mind, just rest..."
Edward said,

"Yes mama, all you have to do is say yes."
and smiled. Nicole looked down at Edward, smiled, took
a sip of her drink, laid her head back and just enjoyed
the attention that was being given to her.
Edward got more rhythmic as his masculine hands
massaged from Nicole's knees down to the tips of her
toes. Edward set down Nicole's left foot and
concentrated on her right foot. Edward put Nicole foot
into both of his hands. He used his right hand and
squeezed in the middle of her foot and with his left hand
pressed right under the ball of Nicole's foot. Nicole said
in a low sultry voice,

"Ummm hmmm right there...just like that
baby...don't stop... that feels so good." She took another
sip of her drink and said,

"Yes baby, rub mama's feet...shit!" At that point,
Edward raised Nicole foot up to his mouth and started
kissing her foot and sucking her toes. Nicole screamed
out, "Ooooh Shit baby that's it!"

Edward continued the motions for a little while longer
and then sensually rubbed up and down Nicole's calf. At
this point, Edward changed positions and continue to
make love to Nicole's feet by just his touch and tongue.
Again, Edward used the same technique on the left foot

that he did on the right. Nicole looked down at Edward
threw back the rest of her drink and asked Edward,
"How many women have you seduce this way?"

Edward looked at Nicole smiled and didn't say a word.
Nicole rested back in the chair and let Edward's hands
take over. The song changed and Edward asked, "Is there
anything else you would like?" Nicole looked at Edward
and replied,
"Come here."
She motioned with her right index finger to come closer
to her face. Edward did as she asked. Nicole rubbed her
left hand across his right cheek and said,
"Kiss Me."
With a bit of hesitation, Edward put his lips up to hers
and did as she asked. As they kissed, Nicole slightly
opened her lips and slid her tongue into Edward's
mouth. The two began to tongue dance for almost a
minute, then Nicole broke the embrace of the kiss saying,

"Thank you so much baabee...I needed that so
badly." Edward said,
"I have enjoyed my time with you. I have to get
back to the party, but can I see you again?" Nicole got up
out of her chair and went over to a section of the room
that contained a drawer. She opened the drawer and
went into a jade green silk pouch. She pulled out a

business card and handed it to Edward. Edward read
the card and said,

"What is the best time and day to call you?"
Nicole smiled and said,

"Mama, will leave that up to you baabee."
Edward got dressed and watched Nicole as she sat
naked in the big leather chair. Nicole sat back in the
chair and watched Edward dress. Once Edward was
dressed, Nicole motioned for him to come close to her.
When he got to eye level with her, Nicole whispered in his
ear,

"No one has ever made me cum like that!"
Puzzled, Edward looked at her and said, "But we didn't
have sex." Nicole smiled and replied,

"Yes...I know...there is more than one way to make
a woman orgasmic... I do hope you call me.
I think we can have a lot of fun together." Nicole kissed
Edward on the cheek. Edward smiled and walked
through the veiled doorway. Nicole said in her mind,

"Now that's a Man!"

TWO

THE FANTASY GETAWAY

Ruby was traveling alone, taking a trip to Las Vegas. She had been looking so forward to this vacation for so long. She had lost so much in her life in the matter of a very short time. It started with her beloved son being falsely imprisoned for a crime of circumstances and was sentenced to 32 years.

Next, she had gotten injured at her job, and had to have surgery on her rotator cuff and was denied short-term disability due to her weasel-like manager Lawrence that needs not be mentioned any further, refused to put in the appropriate paperwork in a timely manner. Due to the lack of income, she lost her house due to foreclosure.

After the surgery, she lost her longtime boyfriend, because she couldn't meet his sexual needs because of her injuries. Right after that, she had a slip and fall and injured her other shoulder and had to have surgery on the other shoulder and not being able to work caused her car to be repossessed.

She then found out her mother was stricken with Alzheimer's dementia and to top it all off, her Rottweiler Tyson that she had raised since he was a puppy had died due to suspicious circumstances.

She was an emotional wreck. All she wanted to do was to have some fun. For her birthday, some friends of hers had took up a collection and got her an all-expenses paid trip to Las Vegas. She had made up in her mind that whatever happened in Vegas would stay in Vegas.

Her friend Annette dropped her off at the airport and before Ruby got out of the car said,

"Now Ruby, don't do anything I wouldn't do." And laughed,

Ruby retorted, "That leaves a whole lot of room to do whatever!" and laughed.

Annette said, "I don't have seven kids for nothing...have fun girl. I will be here to pick you up next week."

"Ok, I love you girl, thanks for everything." Ruby closed the door picked up her luggage and went over to the sky cap.

"Hello, my name is Daron, are you checking a bag today ma'am?" and smiled.

Ruby looked up and saw one of the most attractive men she had ever seen in her life. He stood about 5'10" about 220 LBS. He was dark brown complexioned with an attractive muscular build. Struck by this vision of loveliness,

she stuttered, "Yeeessss!"

Daron continued, "Alright, may I see your ticket?"

Ruby fumbled through her purse and the contents fell out.

"Damn!" Ruby exclaimed.

Daron approached and said,

"Hold on sweetheart, I've got you. Everything is gonna be alright."

He helped her get the contents of her purse and held out her ticket.

"Soooo, you are going to Vegas?!"

Stuttering again Ruby said, "Yeeesss!"

Daron asked, "How long are you staying for?"

Ruby replied while gaining her composure, "A week..."

Daron continued, "That's great! As soon as my shift is over, I hop on a bird myself headed to Vegas. Then my vacation starts... hopefully I will see you in Sin City."

Ruby said, "Well, I will be staying at the Golden Palace."

 Daron stated, "Really! I will be staying at the MGM! Maybe we can hook up and hang out."

Ruby replied, "I would really like that."

 Daron took a luggage identification card, wrote his name and telephone number on the card and said, "My flight gets to Vegas at eight o'clock this evening...call me."

 Ruby looked at the card and said, "I most definitely will." And she went inside the terminal.

As she walked to her gate, she questioned what had just happened. In her mind she asked, "Did I just see the man I have been looking for all of these years?" She had this feeling of being all warm and fuzzy on the inside. She was all smiles while on the plane and even once she made it to her destination. As she stepped off the plane she thought, "So this is Vegas...sin city...I'm not impressed."

As Ruby made it to baggage claim, she spotted a tall lanky white man in a black suit holding a sign that read, Powellson. Ruby walked over to the gentleman and inquired, "Who is the lucky person with my last name?" and smiled. The chauffeur responded, "MS Ruby Powellson ma'am." Shocked, Ruby exclaimed, "That's me!" "I am Giles, your Chauffeur for the weekend...it is all included in your vacation package ma'am."

"No one told me that I was getting a chauffeur driven limousine..."

"You must have good friends ma'am..." replied Giles and then smiled.

"Well ok...I have to get my luggage from baggage claim..."

"That's already been taken care of ma'am." Puzzled, Ruby asked,

"How is that possible?"

"You must have really good friends ma'am..." was Giles's response.

As they walked to the limo, Ruby noticed all of the slot machines and wondered did anyone ever really win big in Las Vegas. Giles and Ruby walked outside of the airport and sitting out was a red on black stretch Lamborghini limousine with the butterfly suicide doors. On the inside was black leather with a full bar. It had a Pro Logic sound system and a partition for privacy.

Awe struck, Ruby thought about a fantasy that she had about making love in the back of a limo and quickly reminded herself that she had no one to share the fantasy with. But she also remembered that this is sin city and whatever happened in Vegas would stay in Vegas. Ruby felt in her pocket and felt the business card and said to herself, "Maybe I won't be alone..." and smiled thinking of Daron.

Ruby got into the limo and Giles closed the door behind her. Giles got into the driver's seat and asked on the intercom,

"Would you like to do some sightseeing, or would you like to go straight to your suite ma'am?"

Unsure, Ruby replied, "What would you suggest?"

"Well Madame, during the day, there are things to see, however the night has the lights..."

With a little apprehension, Ruby said "Ok well, we can go to my suite...I really would like to see the accommodations." "No problem ma'am..." As they drove along, Ruby continued to rub on the luggage card that was in her pocket. She daydreamed about Daron, envisioning his face and his smile. The thought of being with him in the limo made her feel alive again. She took the card out of her pocket and realized it was a coupon for some hot wings at Hooter's. Almost in a frantic frenzy she looked for the card that Daron's information was on and then realized it was in her purse. She began to laugh and thought, "Damn...I've got it bad..."

Ruby pulled out the card from her purse and said, "What the hell!" Ruby took out her cell phone and called the number on the card.

On the first ring, the voicemail picked up and the message said, "This is Daron, leave a message."

Hesitant Ruby left a message, "Hello, this is Ruby, you gave me your number at the airport, you handled my bags...anyway I was hoping when you got to Vegas we could have drinks...give me a call when you get here...bye" as Ruby hung up the phone she thought, "Am I really that desperate for companionship?"

She sat back in the seat of the limo and just enjoyed the ride. They arrived at the hotel and Giles opened the door. Ruby exited the vehicle and waited as Giles retrieved her luggage. A bell boy walked over to the limo and said, "Take your bags ma'am?"

Ruby was distracted by the beauty of the resort. She was captured by the sight of the waterfall and fountains that were in front of the backdrop of palm trees and the reddish brown hue of the mountains.

"Yes...please..." Giles said, "Now Madame, if you need me here is the number to call and I will be there." And he handed her his business card.

"Thank you" as she accepted the card. Ruby walked through the doors of the resort and went to the check-in counter.

"*Good morning, are you checking in?*" "*Yes*"
"*Your name?*"
"*Ruby Powellson...*"
"*Oh...MS Powellson...you are set in the Presidential Suite...here is your key card...you will go around the corner to your right...get on the elevator and take it to the Penthouse floor...the code to get off on that floor is DREAM...are there any questions?*"
Ruby looked around and then said, "No...not right now." Ruby took her key card and followed the directions that were given to her. She got on the elevator and did as instructed. When she got to the Penthouse floor the elevator doors opened and Ruby's heart fluttered.
The place was immaculate. The grand living room had a white marble step down staircase. At the last step of the staircase, the white marble continued to outline the outer edges of the floors. The inner area of the floor was covered with purple and gold carpeting. In the center of the floor was a wooden parquet area. The walls were black marble trimmed in gold. There were these huge crowned moldings that were metallic gold with mirrors all around and in the center of the ceiling was a huge crystal chandelier.
"*Damn...I was not expecting all of this!*"

Ruby walked down the staircase to the center of the room. She was admiring the intricate details of the suite. She looked out of the large picture windows in the living area. There was a magnificent view of the famous Las Vegas strip.

"That is gonna look beautiful tonight..." She said to herself. As Ruby continued to peruse the suite, she opened the enormous two French doors and there was her bedroom. Awe struck, she saw an extremely large canopy bed with satin white veiling draped down the sides in one corner was a full bar and in the other corner was a multi-jet whirlpool. "Oh yeeesss now that's what I'm talking about!" Ruby walked into the bathroom and noticed that the floor and shower area was all stone and Travertine. There were multiple mirrors throughout the bathroom. "Wow!" was the only thought she had. At that very instant, Ruby's cell phone rang.

"Hello"

"Well hello..." "Who is this?"

"I was returning a call...someone called me from this number"

"Daron?"

"Yes, who do I have the pleasure of speaking with?"

"Ummm...this is Ruby...we saw each other at the airport this morning... I left you a message..."

"Oh yeah, I hadn't had the chance to check my messages...I just saw that I had a missed call...I guess you made it to sin city safely...how was your trip?"

"It was ok...a little lonely, but the plane didn't crash..." and Ruby laughed. Daron laughed and responded, "That wouldn't be a good thing if the plane would have crashed, then I wouldn't be able to show you a good time in sin city."

Flattered, Ruby said,"Oh really?...well I am glad it didn't kind of crash either...I kind of like breathing..." and continued to laugh.

Daron inquired,"What do you like to do?...I would like to have an idea of different places that we could go, that you would enjoy." "I am really open and flexible on things must have I like...I am not that hard to please."

"OK...well I know this Middle Eastern spot...they have great food, belly dancers, a whole show...I think you are gonna like it..."

Ruby thought for a minute and asked, "Does everything that happens in Vegas stay in Vegas for real?"

Daron got quiet for a moment, and then said, "If that is what you want..."

Ruby thought for a moment, thinking of her limo fantasy and then asked, "What time does your plane get to Vegas this evening?

Daron replied, "At about 6:30PM...why?"

"Well I was thinking I could pick you and we could go to your spot from there...what is the dress code?"

"It is casual dress...Ok, that will be cool...I have never had a woman pick me up before from the airport...I will get freshened up at the airport...they have showers in the employee's locker room and I have something nice to wear."

"Ok...well, I will see you at about 7:00."

"Ok...I am looking forward to spending the evening with you...well I've gotta run if I am gonna catch that flight for our big date...see you when I get there."

"Ok...see you at 7:00...bye"

"Bye".

Ruby, hung up the phone and her heart started to palpitate. She couldn't believe that she was even thinking about living out her fantasy. Ruby walked over to the whirlpool and turned on the water. She touched the water to measure its temperature. The water was fairly warm.

She began taking off her clothes and looked in the mirrors that lined the bathroom. Ruby admired her body for a minute and thought to herself, "I don't look half bad..."

She pushed the button and the jets turned on in the whirlpool tub. She climbed into the tub and just laid back and relaxed. The bubbles went all across her body and she thought about how wonderful it felt. She had not felt this good in years. After an hour soak, Ruby got out of the bath and wrapped a towel around her. She walked into the living room where she saw her luggage. She grabbed her large bag and went back to the bedroom. She went to the closet and opened the closet doors and to her surprise there hung a full-length black hooded sable coat. "I know this wasn't a part of the trip..." Ruby thought to herself. Ruby took out the coat, dropped her towel and put the beautiful coat on. It was a perfect fit.

Ruby said out loud, "Ok...I have to be dreaming..."
Ruby took off the coat and then paused.
"Maybe it is meant for me to live out my fantasy..."
At that point, Ruby had made up in her mind that
she and Daron were not going out for dinner.
"I am living out my fantasy tonight..." Ruby looked
through her bag and found her six-inch red stilettos.
She put back on the sable coat and stepped into the
stilettos. She admired herself in the mirrors and then
said, "What am I gonna do with my hair?"
Ruby got out her flat irons and began styling her hair
in this intricate pattern that was different from what
she was used to. She called Giles and told him she
would need him to pick her up at about 6:30PM. At
6:30 sharp Giles called to Ruby's cell phone.
"I am in the front Madame..."
"Ok...I will be right down..." Before Ruby left the room,
she looked in the mirror one last time. She smiled,
posed and thought, "Damn I look good!"
As Ruby walked to the elevator, she began to feel a
wave of nervousness. Her thoughts began to race.
"What if Daron doesn't like this?...What if he thinks
I'm a slut?...What am I doing?..."
The doors of the elevator opened and Ruby stepped
in. When the doors opened, she looked out into the
lobby and stepped out of the elevator. As she walked

through the doors of the hotel, she noticed the bell boy and another gentleman look at her and smiled. Ruby smiled but felt like they knew she had nothing on under the coat. Giles was waiting right out front and opened her door. Ruby got into the limo and got comfortable. Giles closed the door and walked to the front of the limo. He got in, closed the door then pushed the button to use the intercom. "Where to Madame?"

"The airport...I am picking up a friend." With that Giles pulled off. While riding, Ruby began having second thoughts, but she also felt like it was too late at this point. Giles pulled into the airport and spoke over the intercom, "What airlines ma'am?"

"I am not sure..." Ruby replied.

Ruby picked up her cell phone and called Daron. "Hello" Daron answered. Nervously, Ruby responded, "Hey...I am here at the airport...where do I pick you up?" "Hey...I landed a little while ago...I'm all showered, dressed and ready to hit the town with you...just pick me up at the employee's entrance."

"Ok...I will come right now... I have a surprise for you."

"Oh really, what's the surprise?" "If I tell you, it wouldn't be a surprise, now would it?" Then she giggled.

Daron let out a little laugh and said, "Yeah I guess it wouldn't." "Ok see you in a few..."
"Ok" and they both hung up.
Ruby pressed the intercom and said, "Giles go to the employee's entrance."
"Ok Madame" Giles maneuvered the limo over to the employee entrance and parked directly in front of the door. Ruby opened the back door and sprung out with great anticipation for Daron to walk out. The seconds seemed like hours, the minutes seemed like days until final there he immerged. Daron was wearing a black pair of pleated slacks with my cream-colored button-down silk shirt. He wore black dress socks and a pair of black and gray snakeskin Stacy Adams. Ruby looked at Daron with pure lust in her heart. She thought right that second, "Hell yeah...Damn he is fine!..."
Daron saw Ruby and the limo and stopped dead in his tracks. Daron was amazed and in awe by the whole sight of Ruby looking so attractive in the beautiful fur coat and the gorgeous red limo parked out waiting for him.
"Is this the surprise?" Daron called out.
Ruby answered, "Part of it" and smiled. "I am a little nervous to see what the rest is...I am blown away...no one has ever did anything like this before...WOW!"

Daron slowly walked over to the limo. Ruby ordered Daron, "GET IN!" and smiled as Daron got into the limo, Ruby began unbuttoning the coat and when she got to the last button, she said, "Here is the rest of the surprise" and opened the coat so only Daron could see her. Shocked, Daron shouted, "Mary Sweet Mother Jesus...Damn...I knew you were fine but Lord have mercy!"

Ruby laughed and then replied, "The Lord don't have anything to do with this...remember we are in Sin City." Ruby climbed into the limo and closed the door. Giles's voice came across the intercom, "Where to Madame?"

"Just drive Giles...take us sightseeing..." "No problem ma'am..."

Daron, still stunned asked, "What made you do this?" Ruby answered, "It has always been my fantasy to pick up an attractive man from the airport, wearing nothing but a fur, high heels and my birthday suit...and to make love in a limo...the making love part will be up to you..." and seductively smiled.

Daron touched Ruby's left cheek with his right hand. Then he cupped the back of her neck, pulled her close to him and kissed her passionately. Ruby's eyes widen for a second in surprise and then closed shut. She believed she was dreaming. Daron put his left arm around Ruby's petite waist and continued kissing her. Ruby began rubbing on Daron shirt, feeling for the buttons and blindly unbuttoned his shirt. When she got to the last button, she broke the kiss and started kissing down his chest.

Ruby climbed onto Daron's lap and the fur came completely off. Daron helped finish taking off his shirt and he caressed her body so lovingly. Ruby worked her hand the button of Daron's pant and unbuttoned it. At that point, Daron said, "Wait...believe me...I want to do this, but I just don't do things like this...I don't know you..."

Ruby, still sitting on Daron's lap said, "Oh yes you do...I am gonna help you remember me...You were number 57 on Julian's high school football team..."

Puzzled Daron said, "Yes I was number 57...how did you know that?"

"Wait, I am gonna help you remember me...do you remember Mrs. Randolph?" "Yes, she was my 12th grade English teacher..."

"Do you remember the skinny little girl that used to come in her room early in the morning right before class started?"

"Yes, Mrs. Randolph's daughter used to come to the room to get her bus money..." The light bulb went off in Daron's head. "...wait a minute...you are Mrs.

Randolph's daughter?!...I knew you was gonna be fine but damn! But wait... how is your last name Powellson?" "Married, divorced, a name change here, a name change there...Powellson...I had the biggest crush on you in high school and you didn't even notice me... so when I saw you at the airport...I had kind of decided then that I was gonna live out my fantasy with you... "

"Well honestly, I noticed you back in high school...but you were Mrs. Randolph's daughter... She made it clear...you were off limits."

 "Well, I am not off limits now..." and she hungrily kissed Daron.

Daron, started to ease off his pants while keeping Ruby on his lap. Ruby reached down grabbed Daron's manhood and stuck the head right at the gates of heaven. "Oh I have been waiting for this!"

Without letting go she guided his penis into her vagina, then put both hands on his chest. She started moving and thrusting her hips up and down against him. Daron began kissing on Ruby's full breasts. Daron licked each nipple, treasuring every lick. Ruby's eyes rolled back in the back of her head as she thrust harder and harder. Then,

Ruby seductively whispered, "So how do you like this ride?...Better than any plane huh?" Daron whispered back, "Baby don't stop, I love this ride..."

Ruby, laughed a little and then screamed, "Shit...Oh shit...Ummm...Yeeeessss...Yeeesss!!!"

Ruby lunged forward, closed her eyes, grabbed Daron around the shoulders, slowed her rhythmic hip motions and just held him. At what seemed like an eternity, Ruby opened her eyes, looked deep into Daron's eyes and said, "You are the man of my dreams..."

 Daron looked back at Ruby and said, "No...you are better than my boyhood fantasy..."

 At that point, Giles asked on the intercom, is there anything specific you want to see ma'am?" Ruby and Daron both laughed and then Ruby answered, "The only thing I want to see is my bedroom suite..."

"I will take you back to the resort Madame..."

"Thank you Giles."

Then Ruby said to Daron, "Soooo are you still staying at the MGM or do you want to stay with me? I know we will have a good time."

Daron proudly and enthusiastically said, "I am surely staying with you...hell I may have a few surprises for you..." and smiled.

Ruby then asked, "Can we get something to eat later? I need a nap..." and smiled back at him. Daron answered, "Sweetheart, you can have anything you want...for this week and hopefully for much longer." Then they both cuddled with each other in the back of the limo under the sable coat and just enjoyed the ride into the future.

THREE

THE BET

'Tonya was a sports fanatic. She could tell you scores and highlights of her favorite teams and the statistical history of teams and players. Tonya had a special love for football because her father had played football professionally.

As a little girl she would accompany her father to some of his practices and all of the home games. Since she never was able to play, she became very good at fantasy football. Now, Derrick was a competitor by nature. He was an All-American athlete. He played football, basketball and baseball in college, but a car accident did what no one on the court, gridiron or diamond could do, end his athletic career.

Tonya and Derrick met at a mutual friend's super bowl party. The two hit it off and would hang out from time to time. The two signed up in the same *fantasy football league together. As the season started, both were doing very well. Both had assembled formidable teams and the season came down to the last day of the season.*

Derrick called Tonya. "Hey girl, what's good?" Tonya responded, "Me of course, how are you?" "Great!... it boils down to tomorrow and we are tied in the standings."

"I am confident...I will win it all."

"Oh, you sound a wee bit over confident...we are tied...Tonya you need to get ready to take over second place darling."

"Second Place?!...baby please...YOU don't have a shot."

"Oh...well if you are that confident, how about a little wager to make things interest?"

"A wager?!...what are we talking about...make it light on yourself."

"OK...no money...something a little more interesting." And then Derrick laughed.

Curious, Tonya inquired, "What is going on in that twisted mind of yours?"

Derrick thought for a few seconds and then said, "If I win, you have to do a striptease for me along with a full body massage."

Tonya responded, "And when I win?"

Derrick thought for a few more seconds and stated, "I will be your slave for a day."

Stunned, Tonya replied, "Are you serious?!...quit playing!"

"I'm serious!"

"How long have you been thinking this up?"

"Since the first time we met...I have always thought you were an attractive woman...but you are always in those big ole sweaters and baggy sweats...I always wondered what was underneath it all...I have always imagined, but now I want to see."

"You really are serious?!"

"Yes Tonya...I know you have known that I have been digging you for a long while...I never said anything because I liked the way we would hang out and have fun. It has been times that I have wanted to just take you in my arms and lay the biggest kiss on you but, I just didn't want to jeopardize our friendship."

"So what changed?"

Derrick took a long pause and replied, "Life is too short...no one is promised tomorrow. Just last year, I lost a cousin to leukemia. He was only 43 and in the past to two months, I have lost an uncle and an aunt and two good friends. I am just not letting anymore time go by without embracing life."

"I know that's right...Derrick, I have liked you for a while...I just didn't know what to say...you are a bit of a ladies man." Tonya began laughing.

"What are you talking about?..." Derrick said with a little snicker, "...I am not a ladies man...I go out on dates...I know my fair share of women...but I am not sleeping with them..." still laughing Tonya continues,

"It's not the sleeping that I am thinking about... even though a bed might be involved..." as Tonya continues laughing. Derrick still giggling says, "I'm a bit of a freak...so I don't necessarily need a bed..." and Derrick lets out a big robust laugh. As Derrick stopped laughing he asks "...So is it a bet Tonya or are you scared?"

"Ok, I will take your bet...but we have to have some limits."

"Ok, what are the limits?"

"If I lose, which I don't think I will, I don't have to get totally nude in this striptease of yours." "What?!...ok...and if I lose, the day of slavery starts at 0700 AM and end at midnight...I don't want you calling me at 2:00 AM having me doing your laundry."

"Ok...bet!"

"Well, girl...I have to run....see you Sunday."

"OK talk to you later."
"Bye"
"Bye".

Tonya sat back in her chair and thought about what just had happened. All through the night she could not get this bet out of her mind. She couldn't get Derrick out of her mind. "Why did he make this bet with me...of all people? I don't know a thing about stripping...why?" she asked herself.

Tonya decided that she would just take a cold shower to get rid of the lusty feelings that she was having about Derrick. Even after the cold water hit the surface of her skin, she stayed mesmerized by the idea of her being intimate with Derrick.

As the hours passed closer and closer to the time of the bet Tonya got more and more nervous. Finally, the day was upon Tonya and she was so nervous that she could not concentrate at all on anything. Tonya, filled with apprehension, called Derrick, hoping to get out of the bet.

"Hello!" Derrick answered the phone in his most masculine voice.

"Ah, hey Derrick" Tonya said in a half confident tone.

"Oh, I know that tone...you want out of the bet..." and Derrick laughed. Tonya's competitive nature came out and she shouted, "Hell naw, come 7:00 AM, you gonna be my bitch."

Derrick continued to laugh. Then Derrick said, "Oh really, I can see you now, shaking that ass getting all naked for me."

Tonya stopped him by saying, "No...we agreed that I wouldn't have to get totally nude."

Derrick stopped laughing and responded, "Tonya, are you ok?... I was just joking...look if you want out of the bet, you can have out...no hard feelings."

Somewhat relieved, but not wanting to appear like a coward Tonya said, "What?!...Are you backing out?"

"Not at all, I just thought you were having second thoughts about this."

"Derrick, I am a woman of my word and a bet is a bet... are you gonna wimp out?"

Derrick got quiet for a minute and then said in an almost intimidating voice, "I will see you at the end of the day!" and hung up the phone.

"Derrick...Derrick!" Tonya cried out. At that point, all Tonya could do was just watch the games and hope that the games played in her favor. As the waning moments of the day ran down it all boiled down to the foot of a kicker. Tonya called Derrick,

"Hello!" Derrick answered the phone in an excited shout.

"Hey...um I was thinking, since we are all tied right now, let's just call the bet a push."

Derrick yelled, "Hell Naw! MS I'm a woman of my word...get ready to shake that ass for daddy!"

Then the announcer says, "...the kick is up and it good.."

Derrick yells in excitement, "YES!!! I can see you now, Dippin' it low, coming up slow and pop pop poppin' that ass...only a miracle can save that ass now!"

Tonya had a tear roll down her face. Just then the announcer says, "...with 12 seconds to go in the game, here is the kick off, and it's a little squib kick... the runner pick up the ball... he is at the 30, he breaks a tackle...he is at the 40...he breaks another tackle..."

Derrick yells, "Come on make a tackle!"

Tonya says, "Yes...go go go!"

The announcer continues, "...the runner is in the open field...and look at that...he could... go... all... the... way! A 70 yard kickoff return for a touchdown as time expired!"

Tonya Screamed, "YESSSS!!!! YESSS!!!....are you ready to be my bitch Derrick?!"

"I ain't nobody's bitch!" Derrick exclaimed. "Well, bitch or not, you are my slave for a day!....so I am expecting you to be here bright and early tomorrow morning...I have a whole lot of shit for you to do...and bring your tools and a change of clothes...you are gonna need them!" Derrick, without saying another word hung up the phone.

The next morning, Derrick was at Tonya's house bright and early at 7:00 on the dot. He rang the doorbell and Tonya came to the door in her big flannel robe with rollers in her hair.

"Damn girl! It's gotta be laws against coming to the door looking like that!"

"Shut up slave, you are to speak when spoken too!"

"You are taking this slave shit a bit too far...so where do you what me to start?" Tonya handed Derrick a bucket with car soap and sponges in it and said, "The car is parked outside of the garage and the water hose is in back of the house waiting for you...the car wax, leather cleaner, dry towels and the car vacuum is in the front seat...hop to it...washed and waxed...cleaned inside and out." Then Tonya closed the door. Derrick stood at the door, let out a sigh and said to himself,

"This is gonna be a long day." Derrick got the hoses and sprayed water on the car. Tonya had poured herself a cup of coffee and watch Derrick in the window as he began washing the car. As Tonya watched Derrick, she saw him take off the sweat suit jacket that he was wearing and all he had on was a white wife beater t-shirt. She saw his muscle ripple as he washed the car and all kind of sexual thoughts raced through her mind. Tonya then went into the living room and watched the morning news. As the morning got hotter, Derrick took off his t-shirt and exposed his well-defined chests and abs. Tonya looked out of the window and said to herself, "UMM HMM, my own private strip show..." and smiled.

Derrick had no idea that Tonya had been watching him. Tonya came out onto the back porch to get a better look at Derrick, but disguised this by saying,

"Even a slave needs a break. Would you like a glass of lemonade?"

Derrick stopped applying the wax to the car and answered, "That would be nice..." As he poured water over his head to cool himself down.

Tonya watched every drop go down his body, making him glisten in the sunshine like a bronze God and for a second, she was mesmerized. Stuttering,

Tonya said, "Here Here Here you go." handing Derrick the glass.

Derrick asked, "Are you ok?"

Still in a stupor but coming out of it Tonya says, "I'm ok...now get back to work!" and walked back into the house. When Tonya got back into the house all she could say to herself was, "Damn he is fine!"

About 30 minutes later, Derrick rang the doorbell. Tonya came to the door in a sheer white blouse with a pair of jeans on and the rollers were out of her hair. Derrick saw Tonya's cleavage through her blouse, and he noticed the way her jeans hugged her hips and he thought to himself, "...damn, she is sexy as hell!" But he didn't express the sentiment to Tonya.

"I'm finished with the car."

"Oh really, let me come check it out."

As Tonya walk passed Derrick, his eyes dropped immediately to her backside and all he thought was, "Baby's got back!" As she looked over the car she would take quick glances at Derrick as he was toweling off the water and sweat from his body. "That's a good job slave." And then she began to laugh.

Derrick looked at her, cracked a smiled and then said, "What's next Mistress?"

Surprised by Derrick getting into the Master Slave persona, Tonya said, "Next up..." as she opened the big door to the garage, "...the garage!...I have marked what I want thrown out and what I want to keep...have at it."

Without another word Derrick began carrying the boxes that were label to be discarded out of the garage. Tonya stood there for a minute to watch Derrick lift the boxes and to see his muscles flex. Caught up in more sexual emotions while looking at Derrick, Tonya announced, "I am going to run some errands, I will be back later...Slave." Then she smiled at Derrick and began to walk away.

Derrick responded, "Ok, see you later...Mistress..." and smiled back at her. About two hours had passed and Tonya pulled up and saw Derrick sitting on the curb holding a towel over his head.

Tonya got out of the car and walked over to Derrick. "Have you finished cleaning the garage?" She noticed blood on the towel and asked, "What happened?"

Derrick looked at her and said, "One of the shelves came apart and hit me in the head."

"Are you oK?" Tonya asked as she took the towel away to see how bad the cut was.

"Yeah, I'm ok...as you see I have finished the garage and I repaired the shelving and you had some wiring issues that could have started a fire...I repaired that too...Mistress..." in an almost sarcastic voice.

"Oh Derrick, the bet is over, you have full-filled your part...I never wanted you to get hurt."

Derrick replied, "A bet is a bet right?...just like you are a woman of your word, I am a man of mine...so what's next Mistress?"

Somewhat saddened by Derrick's response, Tonya said, "Ok...well let me at least clean and bandage the wound...come into the house."

Derrick followed behind Tonya as she opened the door and she told Derrick, "Sit down while I get the first aid kit...a good mistress has to take care of her best slave..." and smiled.

Derrick sat quietly and smiled back. Tonya retrieved the first aid kit from the bathroom. When Tonya returned, she softly caressed Derrick's face as a loving mother would do a hurt child. As Tonya examined Derrick's wound, Derrick could not help but notice Tonya's erect nipples. Tonya placed Derrick's head upon her bosom as if he were her hurt child. The shear silky feeling of Tonya's blouse rubbing against Derrick's head aroused them both, but neither said a word. Tonya cleaned and bandaged the gash.

Afterwards, Derrick looked into Tonya's eyes and said, "Thank you for taking care of my wound...you know...You have a really nice place..."

Tonya "Well, responded, "Thank you...but it's a mess...that's why I have my own personal slave to help clean it up."

"Ok mistress...what's next?" "Household chores!" "Huh?"

"Well, you are gonna start in the bathroom..." Tonya handed Derrick another bucket with all sorts of cleaning supplies and some cleaning rags.

Derrick looked at Tonya, shook his head and said, "Show me the way...Mistress."

Tonya walked down the hallway and opened the door to her right. Derrick looked in and said, "Damn girl, you got drawers hanging all on the shower curtain!" and started laughing.

Tonya, embarrassed not remembering that her underwear was in the bathroom grabbed them and said, "Just get to cleaning slave!...and make sure you clean the queen's throne thoroughly."

Derrick started by cleaning the shower. He ran a small amount of water in the tub and then added cleaning solution. He took out a cleaning brush and started scrubbing the shower tiles. All of the grime from the tiles started running off into the tub. From time to time Tonya walked by the bathroom to see Derrick's progress. For some strange reason, just watching Derrick clean the toilet aroused her.

"How much longer is it going to take you to finish that bathroom slave?"

Derrick looked at her and said, "Do you want it done or done right?...it will be finished when I get finished." And he went back to cleaning.

Still admiring Derrick's attractive body, Tonya responded, "When you finish, I want you to clean and vacuum my bedroom."

"Oh, so I will be one of the lucky few to go in your bedroom?" Derrick said half-jokingly.

Tonya asserted sternly, "You will be the first man, I mean, slave to go into my bedroom!"

"Oh really?!"

"Yeah! A queen don't mess around with the help."

"Ok Queenie, what all do you want me to do in your bedroom?"

"Well, change the linen, dust and polish the dressers, make sure all of my clean laundry is put away...oh yeah...and vacuum...and while you are at it...run me a bubble bath and clean that tub after you are finished."

"A bubble bath?!...I just cleaned the tub!"

"Yes slave...a bubble bath...and you can run the water in the bathtub in my bedroom...and make sure it's not too hot."

Derrick looked at Tonya and said, "You know you are trippin' right, but I am a man of my word."

"And after I am finished with my bubble bath, get yourself cleaned up, change out of those dirty clothes and get ready to prepare dinner." Tonya ordered. Derrick did as he was commanded. Derrick ran the bath water and made sure the water was a little warmer than lukewarm.

Then Derrick added Aphrodite's bubble bath beads and called out, "Mistress, your bath is ready."

Tonya walked into the bathroom in a satin black robe with her hair wrapped up in a white terry cloth towel. Stunned by seeing Tonya in this manner, Derrick stuttered, "Can can can I help you with your robe?"

Tonya smiled and replied, "I think I can handle that, but what you can do is go get yourself cleaned up and get dinner prepared."

Derrick not taking his eyes off of Tonya said, "What would you like for dinner?"

Tonya put her foot into the water and said, "The water feels great...as for dinner...surprise me...now hop to it slave....I am getting hungry."

Derrick responded, "Your wish my command mistress." and walked out of the bathroom, closing the door behind him. As Tonya took off her robe and got into the nice warm bath, she continued to reminisce about seeing Derrick earlier all wet and sweaty. She sat back in the tub hoping that Derrick would come back into the bathroom and offer to wash her back. Derrick went into the other bathroom and took a quick shower. While he was showering, all he did was fantasize about Tonya's robe falling to the floor and her ordering, "Take me my king...I am all yours." At that point, Derrick turned the water on cold to spark him out of his erogenous state. Derrick finished his shower and at the same time Tonya was finishing her bath. As they both walked into the hallway wrapped in towels, they noticed one another and bashfully went back into their respective rooms that they came out of.

"Tonya?" *Derrick called out.*

"Yes?" *Tonya replied.* "Umm, have you gone into your room?"

"No...just tell me when you are in the other room so I can come out in more than just a towel."

"You don't have to put anything on for my account." *and laughed.*

"I bet you would love that." *and laughed herself.*

"Oh, I would really love that!"

"I told you I don't mess around with the help." *and continued laughing.*

Derrick walked into the room where his change of clothes was. "Ok, the hallway is clear."

"Derrick, don't play...are you in the other room?!"

"Yes...and hurry up so I can get in the kitchen...you still want dinner don't you?"

"Yes...I do." *Tonya went through the hallway and went back into her bedroom. She looked into the closet and thought to herself,* "What am I going to wear tonight?" *She pulled out dress after dress and final decided to put on a purple and metallic gold fitted dress with a pair of four-inch black stilettos. Once dressed, she looked at herself in the full length mirror and said,* "Damn I look good!" *She left out of* her bedroom and as she walked into the dining room, she was surprised to see that on the dining room table there was a setting of one plate with two white candles that were lit. There was a maroon napkin with a formal set of flatware on it. In the silver ice bucket was a bottle of chilled Moet champagne. Derrick stepped out of the kitchen in a black tuxedo and a white towel draped across his forearm.

Shocked, Tonya said, "Damn! You clean up very nicely." Derrick walked over to Tonya, took her hand and escorted her to her chair. He then pulled out her chair and said, "Have a seat my queen." Tonya sat down. Derrick lifted up her Waterford lead crystal flute and asked, "Champagne mistress?"

"Oh yes...please." Derrick filled the glass about three quarters of the way full. Then he asked, "May I have a glass with you?"

"Well of course...a good slave deserves a reward...How did you do all of this?"

"Well, mistress...when you ran your errands, I ran some of my own." Then Derrick smiled and turned on some smooth jazz from Tonya's music case. "I wouldn't have thought you would have done all this for me Derrick."

"Why not mistress?...are you not worth it?"

"I am but, I wasn't expecting all of this."

"Are you ready for dinner mistress?"

"I sure am...I could eat a horse!"

"Good, because that is what I have prepared....just joking mistress."

Tonya's face got contorted, then upon hearing the completion of Derrick's sentence, Tonya let out a sigh of relief and smiled.

"I have prepared a garden salad, garlic butter shrimp with angel haired pasta, bone in rib eyed steak and for dessert, chocolate mousse."

"Now that is a meal fit for this queen." Derrick took Tonya's plate and went into the kitchen and a few seconds later he returned. In his hand was Tonya's plate filled with the dinner he had prepared. Derrick placed the plate in front of her and said, "Enjoy your feast mistress."

Tonya took a bite of the garlic buttered shrimp and her eyes rolled in the back of her head. "This is amazing!...I hope everything else is this good."

"Well mistress, I believe it will be."

"Derrick, I mean...slave, who taught you how to cook like this?"

"My mother and father...for the most part."

"Wow!...this is really good."

"Thank you."

"I can't wait for dessert...I love chocolate mousse." Just then the large grandfather clock in the living room sounded, "Dong! Dong! Dong!"

Tonya looked at the clock and said, "Wow, it is already eleven o'clock...time sure flies when you're a queen and you have your own personal slave." Then she let out a giggle. Derrick got up and went into the kitchen. A few seconds later he came back with a dish of the chocolate mousse garnished with a sprig of mint. Derrick pulled up a chair close to Tonya. He took the spoon off of the table, dipped it into the dessert, took out a small portion and fed it to Tonya. Tonya looked into Derrick's eyes, opened her mouth and allowed Derrick to feed her the dessert. Once he placed the spoon in her mouth, she consumed the contents of the spoon, swallowed the dessert and then licked her luscious lips.

Tonya finished her first glass of champagne and then said, "Pour me another glass Derrick." Derrick took out the bottle, poured the glass half full and said, "You called me by my name."

"Yes, slowly but surely I know that you won't be my slave for long and so I have to start facing reality." Then Tonya smiled and threw back the champagne like it was a shot of liquor and said, "Champagne always goes straight to my head and makes me want to be bad...you know Derrick, I have always wanted to be fed dessert in bed by my own personal slave...since I have less than an hour left of servitude, I want my dessert fed to me in my bed." Tonya took the bottle from Derrick and poured more champagne into her glass.

Derrick looked at Tonya and cautiously said, "Your wish is my command mistress."

Derrick then got up and pulled Tonya's chair out for her to get up from the table. Tonya rose from her chair, grabbed her glass of champagne in one hand and the bottle in the other and walked seductively down the hallway towards her bedroom. Derrick followed behind her, holding the dish of chocolate mousse and the spoon. Derrick was entranced in the seductive sashay that Tonya displayed while she walked into her bedroom. Tonya kicked off her shoes and crawled into the bed like a prowling panther. Derrick just watched her. He was so aroused by Tonya's movements but he remained calm, cool and collected.

Then Tonya drunkenly ordered, "Slave! Come here!" Derrick walked over to the edge of the bed. Tonya placed her foot on the crotch of his pant and said, "Well...are you gonna give me my dessert or do I have to order you to do that?!" Derrick asked, "What kind of dessert would you like mistress?"

Tonya took another drink of her champagne and said, "Well I'm damn sure not talking about the chocolate mousse!"

Derrick replied, "No!...I am uncomfortable with this because you have been drinking!"

Tonya reached up and grabbed Derrick by his shirt and pulled him on top of her. Derrick pulling back from Tonya and both loudly and sarcastically said, "I thought the queen didn't mess around with the help?!"

Tonya stopped pulling on Derrick and said, "I'm not drunk Derrick, I know what I am doing."

Derrick thought for a second and replied, "Let me finish feeding you dessert in bed, after that we can see where things go...Ok?"

"Ok...I have always wanted to be served dessert in bed...but then I also fantasied that the dessert would be put all over my body and licked off..." "Hmmm...that sounds interesting." Derrick responded and they both started laughing. Derrick picked up the spoon, dipped it into the chocolate mousse and fed Tonya another spoonful as she lay back on the bed. Derrick took the spoon and dipped it again but only took half as much and placed it on Tonya's right cheek. Then as they looked into each other's eyes, Derrick leaned to the right side where the chocolate mousse was and licked the dessert off of her cheek.

Then Derrick asked, "Did the fantasy begin something like that?"

Aroused, Tonya said, "Not really, but it's a good start." And smiled. Derrick gentle stroked Tonya's left cheek and touched her bottom lip. He looked lovingly into Tonya enchanting brown eyes. Tonya looked back at Derrick and caressed his hand with hers. The two moved closer and closer towards one another. As they moved in unison, both of their eyes closed as they were about to share their first kiss. Just when their lips were about to touch, the grandfather clock sounded, "Dong! Dong! Dong!" Both of their eyes opened and Tonya looked at Derrick sadly. She sighed and said, "You are free...you are no longer my slave..."

FOUR
THE KISS

V eronica was an attractive forty-five-year-old woman that had been married for twenty years. She was a great wife and mother. Upon the children going off to college, the empty nest syndrome kicked in full blast.

Terrance was Veronica's husband. He was a few years older than Veronica but kept himself in pretty good shape for a man in his mid-fifties. The couple was drifting apart and they didn't understand why. They went to marital counseling and did things to try to put the spark back into their marriage but to no avail.

One evening, Veronica was sitting in her backyard patio and noticed an old friend of the family that she hadn't seen in years. His name was

Cliff and he was visiting some family members and happened to spot her out of the corner of his eye. Cliff was younger than Veronica by about four years. You could tell he worked out regularly. He was six feet tall, with a dark complexion and had a great smile.

He walked outside, came to the fence and said, "Hey good lookin', what's cookin'!"

Veronica looked at cliff and answered, "I am the hottest pot on the stove."

"Oh really, well let me touch the pot and see if it burns me."

Veronica smiled, walked over to the fence, smiled and gave Cliff a hug. "How have you been Cliff?"

"Not so good since Sharon passed away...I have been in a real funk lately."

"Oh, I am so sorry to hear that...you all had been together for years...12 or 13 years, right?"

"15...it is so difficult dealing with the loneliness, but hey I will survive...how is Terrance?"

"He is ok...I guess..."

"You guess? You are still together, right?"

"Well, we live in the same house...but that's another story...how long are you in town for?"

"Just a couple of days. I am seeing my mom and some friends...but it seems like everybody has moved away."

"Yeah, people have been moving away from here or dying off...old lady Greendale passed away about a month ago and Mr. Butler passed away three months again. I have been thinking about moving myself."

"You and Terrance or just you?"

"Terrance and I are not doing well in this marriage...I think he is having an affair...he is never home and claims to be working, but I found receipts that shows he was not working, and the receipts were for two."

"Wow, I am sorry to hear that...you two were the perfect couple...I mean picture perfect."

"That is how it used to be..." then Veronica's gaze drifted towards the sunset. Wanting to lighten the mood, Cliff said, "Do you still like jazz?"

"Veronica's eyes lit up. "YES! You know I still do...I have not changed...well, I may have put on a few pounds, but I still love jazz, blues, house..."

"Well, those few pounds you are talking about are hitting you in all the right places."

(Blushing), Veronica replied, "You better watch it now...a girl hasn't been paid a compliment from a man in a long while..." and smiled.

"Oh really, well there are a whole lot more where that came from..."and Cliff smiled back.

"Why did you ask me if I still liked jazz?"

"There is this Jazz revival tomorrow night...I don't want to go alone and I was hoping that two old friends could go together? I don't want to cause any problems between you and your husband, but we have known each other for so long...I didn't think it would be any harm."

Without a second's hesitation Veronica answered, "I would love to go...I never get out of the house and we are two old friends going to hear some Jazz."

"Ok, it starts at 8:00, so would you like to meet at the venue or should I pick you up?"

"I will meet you there...what is the address?"

"It's at the old Barclay lounge on 4th..."

"Oh...yeah! I know exactly where that is...I thought it was shut down?"

"This is the grand re-opening."

"Ok...well I will see you tomorrow."

"I am looking forward to it."

Then Veronica turned and walked back into her house. Cliff stood and watched as Veronica's body moved to and fro. Cliff thought to himself, "That is a sexy woman...I don't know how her man doesn't want her." Then Cliff went inside of his house as well.

The next day at 5:00, Veronica had put on a black satin fitted dress with silver lace across her cleavage area. Her stockings were black fish-net stockings with silver glittered high heeled shoes to match. Her makeup consisted of white eye-liner on her eyelids and one-half inch eyelashes. Her caramel complexion had a sublime glow because she was so excited to be going out with a male companion.

As she thought about the evening, she wondered what the evening would be like. She remembered that she had been attracted to Cliff for years, but she never let him or anyone else know this because in the past, they were both happily married. As Veronica was getting dressed, Terrance walked into the bedroom. "Wow!" Where are you going all dressed up?"

"Out!" is all that Veronica said.

"Really?!...out with who?"

"What do you care? Don't you have to work or go out with God knows who or something?"

"What is that supposed to mean?"

"Nothing Terrance..."

"NO! You meant something by that."

"I am not going to argue...I am going out to hear some Jazz...It's not like you take me out anymore nor do anything else with me."

"We went out two weeks ago!" "To the movies, big deal...but you can go spend $200 on a meal with whomever right?"

"What?"

Then Veronica walked over to the dresser and opened it. She went into the small compartment in the dresser and pulled out a receipt. "You and someone else...not me... spent $200 on a meal when you were supposed to be at work...I have never questioned you about anything...but I have questions. So tonight, you are gonna have questions about me."

Terrance picked up the receipt and said, "This was business!"

"C'mon Terrance, I am not a genius, but I am not a fool either."

As Veronica began walking away, Terrance grabbed her by the arm. "No! It was business!"

"Get your Goddamn hands off of me!" Terrance let Veronica go. As Veronica walked out of the door, she looked back at Terrance and eerily said, "I want a divorce."

Shocked, Terrance said nothing. Veronica walked out of the door. A grin went across Veronica's face as she thought about seeing Cliff. Veronica got into the car, started the car, reved up the engine and peeled rubber. She felt like the weight of the world was lifted off of her shoulders. Veronica thought to herself, "I have wanted to do that for a long time..." As Veronica arrived at the lounge, she noticed the long line to get in. She thought to herself, "...it's a nice crowd."

Veronica pulled up to the parking lot. The valet walked over to her car and said, "Name please?" Veronica looked at the valet and said, "Veronica Thompson..." The valet looked at his list and said, "Ok Mrs. Thompson, when you leave the lot, go straight to the door, you don't have to wait in line...here is your ticket for parking...have a great time..." and smiled at her.

Veronica took the ticket and walked to the front of the line as she was directed to do. When she got to the door, she asked the doorman, "How much does it cost to get in?" The doorman replied, "Name please?" "Why? I just want to know the cost for tonight's event?" "Well, the owner told me to ask every attractive woman her name and if it matched the name on my sheet direct them to the V.I.P. section. So please ma'am, tell me your name."

"Veronica Thompson." "You are fine!" "Excuse Me!" "Mrs. Thompson, it was a compliment." "It's MS..." "Ok...go through the doors, hang a right, go up the stairs and you will see the V.I.P. section." "Ok...Thanks and thanks for the compliment..." and gave a quasi-smile. Veronica followed the doorman's instructions and arrived at the V.I.P. section. She looked inside the door of the room but there was no one inside. She walked in and took a sit on the large plush brown leather throne type chair that was in the room.

A few seconds later, a waiter walked in and asked, "Can I get you something to drink?"

"Yes please, a frozen strawberry margarita." "That is coming right up ma'am."

As the waiter walked away, Veronica could hear the music start to play. The music was slow and smooth. It was just the right rhythm to slow dance to. Just then Cliff walked through the door. Veronica's heart almost skipped a beat. Cliff was dressed in a black silk collarless shirt with a pair of black slacks and black and silver cowboy boots.

"Hello, beautiful!" Cliff said as he walked over towards Veronica.

"How do you like the V.I.P. section?"

All smiles, Veronica answered, "It is all good."

"That is what I like to hear." Cliff replied. Veronica inquired, "So do you know the owner? I am not used to getting into V.I.P. sections"

"Well, I think I know the owner fairly well." "Ok...the music sounds great." Just then Cliff gave Veronica a hug and said, "I have been looking forward to that since our hug yesterday."

"Oh really, well I have been needing a hug since yesterday. I confronted Terrance about his cheating."

"Oh...what did he say?" "He denied it...said it was business."

"How do you feel about the whole thing?"

"I told him I wanted a divorce."

"Really...I am sorry that is happening to you...well I hope that I can make you feel better." Just then the waiter came in with Veronica's drink.

"Here is your frozen strawberry margarita ma'am."

"Thank you." "Mr. Chambers, can I get anything for you sir?"

"Scotch...neat." Impressed Veronica said, "Mr. Chambers?...What?! They know you like that up in here?"

"Knowing the owner has its privileges..." and Cliff smiled.

"The music really sounds good up here Cliff, I can see why this is V.I.P."

"The band is really good and the sound system ain't to shabby either." As Veronica took a sip of her drink, she could tell it had plenty of alcohol. "Damn! They must have put a whole bottle of tequila in this drink... two or three sips of this and I may be down to do anything."

"Naw, you are too much of a lady to do... Anything!..."

"Well, you are right, but I really will let my hair down a little." Veronica walked back over to the large chair and sat down. Cliff followed behind Veronica, but remained standing.

Right then the waiter walked in and said, "Here is your drink Boss."

"Thanks Manny..."

"Anything else Boss?..."

"Not right now Manny."

The waiter turned around and walked away.

"Boss?!." Veronica shouted.

"It's a figure of speech..."

"Yeah right!...anyway..." Cliff smiled, looked into Veronica's hazel green eyes and said, "Would you like to dance?"

Veronica threw back the rest of her drink and said, "I would love too." Veronica arose from the chair.

Cliff held out his hand and Veronica took it. Cliff wrapped both arms around Veronica's waist and held her closely.

Veronica smelled Cliff's cologne and commented, "You really smell good...what are you wearing?"

He replied, "I went ole school tonight...Drakkar."

"That smell is doing something to me...I don't know if it's the cologne or the alcohol, but I feel like talking...or more like confessing."

"Confessing?...Confessing what?"

"Cliff, I have been attracted to you for years...I never said anything because we both had significant others. Now that we don't, I just feel like I have to get this off of my chest."

"I have felt the same way. I would see you with your family and I would wonder what things could have been like with us as a couple."

As the two swayed to and fro to the beat of the music the two could feel the rhythms of each other's heart beats. Cliff pulled away slightly and asked, "Are you a good kisser, because I think that you are and I know that I am."

Veronica said, "I will just have to see for myself." And the two simultaneously kissed each other with so much passion, that ecstasy filled the air to a point that they totally forgot that they were in a public place. Their tongues intertwined in a sublime rhythmic dance. Their lips pressed to one another like conjoined twins. The kiss lasted a little more than an instance but to them, the kiss was never ending.

As they broke the embrace of the kiss, they continued to hold one another. Cliff commented, "Your lips are so soft."

Veronica replied, "So are yours...that kiss is exactly how I imagined it would be."

"Have you imagined about anything else?" "Yes, but that will take us some time to get too." The two smiled, kissed each other again and that kiss continued until the end of the night.

FIVE

TELEPHONE INTIMACY

(No Names/No Faces/ Just an intimate conversation)
(The Telephone Phone Rings) Ring...Ring...Ring

M: *Hello...*

F: *Hey You!*

M: *How are you doing?*

F: *I'm Ok, Just dealing with some things.*

M: *What kind of things?*

F: *You Know...some female needing some THINGS!*

M: *Pinned up type of things? Been a while huh? (Starts to laugh)*

F: *Yes! Them kind of things...and yes, it has been a while. (Starts to laugh)*

M: *Can I Help?*

F: *I don't think so. You are too far away.*

M: *I can still help...*

F: *Oh Really?!... I didn't know it was that long. (Starts to laugh again)*

M: *Oh you've got Jokes! See for that I shouldn't help you, but since you are my girl...(Starts to laugh again)*

F: *You don't have to do me any favors...(Still Laughing)*
M: *This will be a favor you will never forget.*

F: *Oh Really?! Ok...What do I have to do?*

M: *First, I need you to keep an open mind. Secondly, I need you to get out your vibrating toy...*

F: *Boy! My toy doesn't do it for me anymore!*

M: Trust Me!

F: You know...my baby was born because of "Trust Me!"

M: (Laughs again) Well, I don't think you have to worry about that happening in this situation.

F: Anything Else?

M: Yeah, get comfortable, get a glass of wine and get naked!

F: What?! Are you serious?

M: Trust Me!

F: Ok...Hold on a minute... (2 minutes goes by) Ok, I'm back. I have done everything that you asked...Now what?

M: Just listen to the sound of my voice...what I want you to do first is lay back on the bed and close your eyes. Just listen to the sound of my voice as I take you on this intimate get away. Now, take a sip of your wine and turn on your toy. Take another sip of your wine and put your toy under your right earlobe. Take another sip of your wine.

F: (Giggles) That tickles...

M: Next, ease your toy across your cheek and along the side of your neck. Then gently move it from your neck to your right nipple. Make small circles on the tip of your nipple, then slide your toy across to your left breast and make small circles on the tip of your left nipple. Take it nice and slow...there is no rush. Next, as you listen to my voice, imagine being kissed.

Now place your toy in the place where you just thought of being kissed. Hold it in that spot until I count to five. 1,2,3,4,5. Now glide your toy down the right side of your body.

Once you get to your waistline, move your toy to the left side of your body. Using your toy, move it up the left side of your body very slowly.

Now again, imagine being kissed, but this time, on the lips. In your mind, feel the hard press of lip to lip, right then the lips soften. Next imagine your lips slightly parting and you feel another's tongue. Hold that thought as I count backward from five. 5, 4, 3, 2, 1.

Now, take your toy and gently guide it down the middle of your chest to your navel. Circle your navel slowly. Then take your toy and run it across your inner right thigh. From your inner thigh, guide your toy to your right knee and then switch to your *left knee and then run your toy from your left knee up to you left inner thigh.*

Next, gently place your toy slightly above your special place. Let your toy rest there until I count to ten.

One, ease your toy slowly inside you. Move it back and forth.

Two, move your toy up and down and in and out.

Three, hold your toy in you and turn it slowly.

Four, pull it out slightly and then put it back in.

Five, take it out and rub the outside and put it back in.

Six, Move your toy back and forth and up and down.

Seven, keep going in and out.

Eight, keep going back and forth, In and out...faster now, in and out.

Nine, hold your toy right there. Keep holding it, hold it, that's it right there! Ten!

F: *Ooooh yes! Damn! Yesss...Ummm...Yesss...That's what I needed! Whew! Damn that was incredible!*

M: *How do you feel?*

F: I can't describe how I feel...

M: Well, I hope I helped you with them things (Starts to laugh)

F: You did more than helped!

M: Hopefully, next time, I can be there to watch...

F: Or join in, but we will have to see (Starts to laugh)

M: Ok, I will talk to you soon (laughs)

F: OK! Thanks again for all of your help.

M: No problem, it was my pleasure.

F: No, it was mine.

M: Bye Girl!

F: Bye!

SIX

CAR TROUBLE

Rhonda-Lynn was an attractive 5' 6", 145lb, Caucasian female and had a perfect Marilyn Monroe hour glassed figure. She had natural honey gold blond shoulder length hair that was in a uniquely crinkled hairstyle. Her eyes were a grayish jade green hue. She was a hair stylist at a local hair salon, but she had ideas of one day owning her on styling Salon.

It seemed like every other day something bad would happened. In just the past few days, two appointments had cancelled, along with finding out a close friend had been diagnosed with ALS, not to mention that her rent was due and she did not have the money to pay it. Not only that, a once in a lifetime opportunity to meet with a group of prominent political figures who could have brought her closer to her dreams had slipped through her fingers due to a scheduling conflict. It was like Rhonda-Lynn was hexed. It seemed that every time she would have an opportunity to get ahead, something negative would happen to her.

One day, just the opportunity that she was looking for presented itself. Rhonda-Lynn received a call from an agent that had notice her work and had connections with universal studios. She was going to have the opportunity to do hair and makeup for a selection of well-known supermodels.

As she gathered the tools of her trade, she felt so optimistic. She got out to her car and packed everything she needed, started the engine and began to drive.

As she was driving along, bang...pop...wobble ...wobble...wobble...wobble. Rhonda-Lynn pulled over to the side of the road and realized that her tire had a blow-out. "Damn! Why can't I get a break...Murphy's Law rears its ugly head again!" She shouted.

As she starts to call triple A, she realizes that her phone was dead. "Damn! Why do these things keep happening to me?!" and she began to cry. Just then a tow truck pulled up. The driver got out the truck. He was a large statured man standing at 6'4", weighing a robust 260 pounds of solid muscle. He was maybe ten percent body fat. He had a mahogany brown complexion and sported a bald head with a neatly trimmed goatee.

The driver said in a deep baritone voice, "Good morning...It looks like you had a blowout...by the way, my name is Travis...You need any help ma'am?"

Rhonda-Lynn looked at Travis and wiped the tears from her eyes and responded, "Hello, I am Rhonda-Lynn, I really need some help, but I am broke as hell and I really have an important meeting that I have to get to."

Travis looked at the tire and said, "I'll tell you what, let me load up your car, then I will take you to your appointment. After dropping you off, I will fix your tire and bring your car back to you...How does that sound?"

Rhonda-Lynn thought for a minute and said, "That sounds great, but I don't have any money and I don't like owing anyone."

Travis smiled and responded, "Sometimes if you put positive energy in the atmosphere, positive things will come back to you...think of this as my way of putting positive energy in the universe."

Stunned, Rhonda-Lynn replied skeptically, "And I won't owe you anything?"

Travis continued to smile and said, "Not a dime, unless you want to be put on a Karma layaway payment plan..." and started to laugh.

Rhonda-Lynn smiled and said, "That is the sweetest thing that has ever happened to me." And she smiled.

"Ok... get what you need out of your car for your meeting so I can load your car up."

"Ok!" Rhonda-Lynn began to get her supplies out of her car. As she gathered her things for her meeting, she looked at Travis and began to think to herself..."I have never been attracted to black men, but he looks good."

Travis started putting the hooks and straps onto Rhonda-Lynn's car.

As he finished, Travis walked over to Rhonda-Lynn and said, "Your car is all loaded up." Travis opened that passenger door and said, "Your chariot awaits."

Rhonda-Lynn smiled and said, "Why thank you." Rhonda-Lynn climbed into the truck and Travis closed the door behind her. Travis walked to the other side of the truck and the door was opened for him by Rhonda-Lynn. Travis climbed into the truck and said, "Why thank you!"

Rhonda-Lynn smiled back and said, "I am putting positive energy back into the atmosphere."

Travis responded, "Well that is great...where are we headed?"

"Universal Studios!" Rhonda-Lynn answered. Travis stated, "You know, I have always wanted to go there, but never have made the time."

Rhonda-Lynn remarked, "Well, you are headed there now...make the most of it."

Travis thought for a moment and then said, "I am going to do just that...after I fix your tire and bring your car back, I am going to explore Universal Studios...when you finish your meeting would you like to join me?"

Rhonda-Lynn thought for a moment and then said, "Of course I would love to because this will be my first time seeing Universal Studios as well, but I really don't know how long my meeting is going to last."

"Ok then, let's play it by ear."

"Ok!"

Then Rhonda-Lynn went into her purse and got out a business card and handed to Travis.

"My phone is dead, but here is my business card." Travis took the card, looked at it and said, "If you want, I can charge your phone."

Rhonda-Lynn exclaimed, "You know you are a real life saver or should I say my sexy knight in shining body armor!" and smiled at Travis.

Travis slightly blushed, smiled and then said, "Just plug your phone into the charger in front of you."

Rhonda-Lynn plugged the phone into the charger. After a few moments of charging, the phone came on and there was a message. Rhonda-Lynn checked the message and it said, "This message is for Rhonda-Lynn, this is Mr. Sherwood, the agent that you were supposed to meet at Universal Studios. Due to a scheduling conflict, we have to change the meeting time and date. The meeting will take place tomorrow at 11:00 AM. Sorry for any inconvenience."

After hearing the message Rhonda-Lynn said, "Well, looks like Universal Studios is out!" "What happened?" inquired Travis.

"My meeting was cancelled for today."

"Ok, well at least I can get your tire fixed and you can enjoy the rest of your day."

"Well at least the next meeting is set for tomorrow at 11:00AM."

"Well then, let's get your car taken care of." As they pulled up to the garage, Rhonda-Lynn noticed a multitude of car and motorcycle racing trophies in the window. Travis parked the truck, got out of the truck and began unhooking Rhonda-Lynn's car.

Rhonda-Lynn looked at the trophies and said, "What are all of these trophies for?"

Travis looked and then responded, "Those are from a previous life...just a reminder of what could have been."

Rhonda-Lynn walked through the door and saw all kinds of certificates and awards hanging on the wall. As she continued to admire it all, she said, "Do you still race?

Travis changed the subject, "What kind of tire do you want on your car?"

Rhonda-Lynn continued to admire the awards and responded, "It doesn't matter, as long as it rolls." and started to laugh.

Travis laughed and said, "Well, I could give you a square tire, but it would give you terrible gas mileage."

They both laughed at the statement. Then Rhonda-Lynn inquired again, "So are you going to tell me about your racing career?"

Travis glanced towards the trophies, then looked at Rhonda-Lynn and said, "I promised someone that I wouldn't race anymore..." Travis's voice trailed off... then he asked, "Have you ever loved something so much and you had to give it up?"

Rhonda-Lynn thought for a second and said, "Yeah crack and my baby..." and began laughing. Travis's face went stoic.

Then Rhonda-Lynn said, "Travis, I was joking...I have never done drugs and I have never been pregnant, let alone had a baby... But I just wanted to see your reaction...but to answer your question...I have never really gotten attached to anything or loved anyone because things and people never stay in my life for long. I lost my parents when I was seven...then I stayed with my grandmother until I was fourteen...when she passed away, I moved in with an aunt and that was not the best of situations, but it helped me avoid getting into the Child Welfare system. I stayed there until I graduated from high school and I have been on my own ever since...It just seems like I am Jinxed because every time things start going well, something bad happens and I lose it...who did you make the promise to that you wouldn't race anymore?"

Travis thought for a moment and then responded, "My wife!" Rhonda-Lynn face got contorted and she stared at Travis and yelled, "Your Wife?!"

Travis cracked a smile, started laughing and said, "I wish I had a camera, because that look on your face is classic! I have jokes too...but actually I promised my older brother that I would not race anymore...it was on his death bed after he had crashed in a street car race...and before you ask...no I have never been married and I don't have any kids."

Relieved, Rhonda-Lynn asked, "Well, do you at least still ride your motorcycle?"

"I ride from time to time...do you ride?" Travis replied.

"Well not really...my dad used to put me on his bike and he would take me places on it when I was little...I used to love those times spent just me and him...it was the speed that I loved...it was a real adrenaline rush." Travis then inquired,

"How did your parent die?" "In a snow storm...my mom and dad were on a weekend getaway in the Sierra Nevada Mountains and a blizzard shut down the roads and an avalanche buried them alive...when they were found, their bodies were joined together."

"Joined together?" Travis asked. "Yes...joined together!" "Do you mean what I think you mean?" Travis questioned.

"Yes Travis, they were making love when they died..." Travis responded, "

This isn't another one of your jokes or to see how I would react is it?"

"No Travis...that is the Truth." Rhonda-Lynn affirmed.

Then Travis commented, "Damn! What a way to go! To die making love to the one you love...I hope I can go out like that... "

Then Rhonda-Lynn said suggestively, "Yeah, we could come and go at the same time!" and she began laughing.

At hearing Rhonda-Lynn laugh, Travis began laughing also.

Then Travis made a suggestion, "Let's take a ride on the black python?"

Rhonda-Lynn looked and Travis and said, "What kind of ride are you talking about?" and smiled seductively.

Travis responded, "Get your mind out of the gutter...a ride on my bike." And then he chuckled and continued. "I call it the black python because obviously it's black and I have had it stretch out longer than any bike around here."

Rhonda-Lynn said, "I thought you would never ask...I would love to...it would make me remember happier times in my life."

Travis motioned with his hand for Rhonda-Lynn to follow him. He walked towards the back of the garage and Rhonda-Lynn followed behind him.

In the very back of the garage was an object covered with a long black tarp. Travis pulled off the tarp and there stood a long stretched Black and Chrome Suzuki Hayabusa motorcycle. Rhonda-Lynn looked at the motorcycle with amazement and said, "That's a nice bike."

Travis took the motorcycle key out of his pocket and put it into the ignition. When the bike started, different color lights in the ground effect kits lit up and the bike looked like an exhibit show all to itself. Travis climbed on board and revived the engine. Then he walked the bike over to the garage door and pushed a button on the wall and the large garage door went up.

Travis looked over at Rhonda-Lynn and said, "Get on!" Rhonda-Lynn slowly approached the bike. As she approached it, a sense of excitement rushed *through her body as she thought back to her and her father's rides together.*

As she straddled the bike, she wrapped her left arm around Travis's mid-section and she could feel his rock hard abs. As she got comfortable sitting in the seat, Travis reved up the engine a few more times and the vibrations rushed through Rhonda-Lynn's lady parts.

Rhonda-Lynn never having felt that pulsating sensation before exclaimed, "Oh Shit! Is that how every ride is going to feel?" and with a devilish grin

Travis turned back and looked at Rhonda-Lynn and said, "Which ride are you talking about?"

Rhonda-Lynn looked back at Travis, smiled and replied seductively, "I believe all of our rides are gonna be great...whether on two wheels or no wheels at all...It looks like my luck in life is changing for the better."

Travis stated, "The universe is a positive beautiful place." She wrapped her other arm around Travis's waist and kissed him on the cheek. Travis turned from Rhonda-Lynn and looked at the street. He pulled out of the garage slowly and sped off into what looked to be a very positive future together.

From the Senses to Sensuality

SEVEN

THE TIGRESS

*I*ris was a prosecuting attorney for a year after she graduated Magna Cum Laude from Harvard Law then she switched to the more lucrative defense side and was undefeated in the courtroom.

Her colleagues called her, "The Tigress" at the courthouse because she was beautiful, aggressive and deadly in the courtroom jungle as well as in all of her other endeavors. She was 5'2" and weighed about 120lbs. She was also a third degree black belt in karate. She had long curly thick black hair, along with dreamy brownish hazel eyes and she had smooth dark chocolate complexioned skin. Iris reveled in beating her competition, especially her male counterparts.

In her Karate tournaments, she would compete against the men and would have great success against them. Iris was just as aggressive in her personal relationship. Someone once told her that she would be one hell of a dominatrix if she ever wanted to give up being an attorney. Iris would go to local bars and prowl the scene for her catch of the night. Her mantra was, "I am successful, rich and I don't need anybody but me...I get what I want when I want it...and no one better get in my way."

One night she went into one of her spots that she liked to frequent after a long day in court. She walked up to the bar and said, "Bartender...Whiskey...neat!"

The bartender looked at her and said, "Are you sure? A pretty little thing like you may not be able to handle a drink like that."

Iris looked at the bartender and said, "You must be new here...well let me set you straight on a few things, first off, don't let the small frame fool you. I can handle my liquor and myself very well, secondly, I know and get what I want when I want it and third, if you can't take my order, get me someone that can!"

The bartender stepped back and replied, "I am new here ma'am and I didn't mean no harm... here let me make it up to you. Your drinks are on the house this evening."

The bartender poured the first drink and handed it to Iris. She looked at the drink and drank it quickly and said, "Make the next one a double!"

Shocked, the bartender said, "Can I ask a question?"

Iris said, "You already did... but what is your next question?"

the bartender replied, "Are you drinking to relax or are you drinking to get drunk?"

Iris responded, "Is there a difference?"

"Well yeah, if you are trying to relax, I have drinks that will do just that, if you are trying to get drunk, I can make you a drink that will take you there much faster than whiskey."

"Ok, I am drinking to get drunk, what would you suggest?" asked Iris "

A Caribou Lou!" replied the bartender. "A what?!" Iris shrieked.

"A Caribou Lou!" the bartender answered.

"What's in it?!" Iris demanded. "151 Rum, Malibu Rum and Pineapple Juice...want to try it?" The bartender asked.

"Sure...why not?!" Iris answered. The bartender made the drink in a highball glass and was about to add ice when Iris ordered, "No ice!"

"No ice it is." said the bartender.

Iris looked at the drink and threw it back as if it was a shot. "Not bad!...give me another one and don't hold back on the 151."

Shocked, the bartender said, "One more coming up."

Just then a familiar face walked through the door. He stood about 6'3" and weighed about 215lb. He had a body type similar to the basketball player Derrick Rose, but a touch heavier. He was caramel complexioned with raven black wavy hair and his hair was cut in a bald fade. He had honey brown eyes with deep cheek dimples. He was slightly bow-legged and had straight pearly white teeth.

Iris called out, "Keith...Keith Peters!?"

"Iris The Tigress Reynolds!...How have you been?" Keith asked.

"I am good, just having a few drinks...what are you doing around here?" responded Iris.

"Just in town for a couple of days to handle some business...I have not seen you since law school...that was two years ago."

Iris smiled and said, "Has it been that long?...here sit down and let me buy you a drink."

"Cool, a beautiful woman offering to buy me a drink is very rare for me."

Iris yells, "Bartender, two of those Caribou Lou things!"

The bartender answered, "Coming up."

Iris turned to Keith and said, "You are still looking good...you know you are the one that got away."

Keith stared at Iris and said, "Got away?! What do you mean?

You were the one that didn't want any, how did you put it, no emotional attachments. Your plan was to be the youngest partner at Sparks, Boyce & Associates..."

Iris cut Keith off and stated, "Now it Sparks, Boyce, Reynolds and Associates...I made partner last year."

Keith responded, "Wow...that is fantastic! So you have accomplished everything you wanted right?"

Iris commented, "Well, like I said, I didn't get you."

Keith blushed and said, "You just wanted another notch on your purse belt."

Iris asked, "What is wrong with a woman that goes after what she wants?"

Keith answered, "Absolutely nothing, but I wanted to be more than one of your conquest...I remember some of the guys you left in your wake. One in particular that comes to mind was Jamal Cooper."

"Jamal Cooper, Jamal Cooper?!" Iris tried to remember back as she took a sip of her drink.

Keith took a sip of his drink and continued, "Yeah, Jamal Cooper...You messed his head up so bad he dropped out of school and became a handy man...is it true you two got busy and afterwards you kicked him out of your apartment naked?"

"Ooooh SMALL Jamal Cooper!...yeah now I remember...He should have become a trash collector because he was garbage in his classes and in bed...C's in the classroom, F's in the bedroom and SMALL is an understatement!"

Keith looked at Iris and said, "Damn girl! You are hard on the brother aren't you?"

Iris retorted, "I call them as I see them! Always have, always will!" and as Iris finished her statement, she slammed the rest of her drink.

Keith took another sip of his drink and then there was an awkward silence.

The bartender walked up and asked, "Anything else?"

Iris looked at Keith, and said, "One more for me, how about you Mr. Man?"

Keith looked at the bartender and said, "I'm good thanks."

Iris gazed at Keith for a moment and said, "If you're scared, say you're scared."

Keith looked at Iris and asked, "How did you get here?" Iris replied, "I walked...I stay right down the street."

Keith stated, "Good because I would hate for you to get behind the wheel in your condition."

Iris with her speech slightly slurred stated, "What do you mean in my condition?!"

Just then she stood up and sat back down and yelled, "Bartender...that last drink got me, what do I owe you!"

Keith stood up. He looked at Iris and said, "Let me walk you home." The Bartender whispered in Keith's ear, "It's on the house...just make sure she gets home safely."

Keith replied, "I will...thanks a lot." Keith put his arms around Iris's waist and helped her stand up.

As they walked through the door Iris said, "You better not try anything, I can still fight dammit!"

Keith responded, "I bet you can..."

As the two walked down the street, Iris asked, "Keith, do you remember that time we went to that frat party and we kissed?"

Keith responded, "Well, I remember you trying to kiss me and I told you I don't do anything with a woman that is inebriated..." Iris continued,

"After all of this time, I still want to kiss you..."

Keith replied, "And it seems you are inebriated every time you want to kiss me...well if you feel the same way when you sober up, we will see."

As they walked up to Iris's front door Keith asked, "Where are your keys?"

Iris responded, "In my purse...wait I will get them." Then she poured everything out of her purse onto the ground and then propped herself against the wall of the doorway and said, "There they are..."and starting laughing in a drunken manner.

Keith picked up the keys and unlocked the door. He then picked up the contents of Iris's purse and placed them back in her purse. Iris watched Keith put the contents back in her purse and asked in a drunken slur, "Keith, do you like me?"

Keith replied while placing his arms around her waist to help her through the door, "Iris, let's get you in the house."

"No Keith, I want an answer now!"

Keith looked at Iris and said, "You don't get everything you want when you want it and I will answer that question when you are sober and can remember the answer that I will give you. Now let me help you into the house."

Iris snatched away from Keith's embrace and yelled drunkenly, "I don't need your gat damn help! I don't need nobody! Get the hell away from me!" as she said that, Iris stumbled through the front door and fell to the floor of the vestibule.

Keith looked at Iris for a moment and reached down to help her up. "Come on Iris, let me help you up."

Iris looked at Keith and she had tears in her eyes. Keith put his arms around Iris and lifted her in one swoop. Then he laid her on the large suede gray lounger that sat to the right of the entrance way of the parlor. Within minutes Iris had passed out sleep. Keith sat on the recliner that was across from where Iris was sleeping. Keith watched Iris as if he were her guardian angel. Within a few minutes Keith had fell asleep. The next morning Keith awoke and saw that Iris was still asleep. Keith explored Iris's home and noticed the beautiful art work that she had hanging on her walls. Then he spotted a glass and brass curio stand where he noticed a picture of Iris from college.

Right next to it was a picture of himself and Iris from the frat party that they had talked about the night before. Keith looked over to where Iris was sleeping and said to himself, "Those were some good times." Keith walked into the kitchen and went directly to the refrigerator. When he opened it, He noticed not much in there. Keith took out eggs, cheese and tomatoes. Then he looked in the cabinets and found a glass bowl and some spices. As Keith prepared omelets, he thought about the times he and Iris had spent together. "Damn! She doesn't have any bread. She is living like she did in college." and began chuckling.

After Keith finished preparing breakfast, Keith went into the living room and walked over to Iris and nudged her softly saying, "Iris? It's morning... wake up sleepy head."

Iris opened her eyes and smiled upon seeing Keith. She stretched and then said, "Hey handsome."

Keith smiled and asked, "So how did you sleep?" "Like a baby...hey...something smells good." replied Iris.

Keith stated, "Well that would be breakfast...are you hungry?"

Iris sat up and said, "Well I could eat." "Well let's eat...go wash your hands and face...would you like to eat in the kitchen or here?"

"In the kitchen will be fine." Iris went into the bathroom and washed out her mouth. Then she washed her face and hands. Iris walked out of the powder room and walked into the kitchen and saw that Keith had placed two plates with silverware on the island and had lit two candles.

Surprised, Iris thought for a few seconds and then said, "Keith, before we have breakfast, I need to know something, how do you feel about me?"

Keith looked into Iris's eyes and said, "After all of these years and after all the things we have been through, you don't know?" Iris thought again, smiled and said, "Why can't you ever give me a straight answer?" "Because my actions over all these years should tell you how I have always felt about you."

Then without saying another word Iris grabbed Keith by the back of his neck, placed her lips next to his and slid her tongue inside his mouth and began flickering it like a cobra's. Keith began kissing Iris back and pulled her closer to him. Iris then started playing with Keith's tongue in a way that made him feel like they had been lovers for years. Iris broke the kiss and said, "I am not inebriated now, what's up?

I have wanted you since college and I can surely tell by that bulged in your pants that you have wanted me too. So let's finally do the damn thing!"

Keith looked at Iris, pulled away and said, "Iris, let's have breakfast first and talk about this...yes I want you and have wanted you, but I have always wanted more from you than just sex."

Iris looked into Keith eyes and said, "I know that, and I think that has been the biggest turn on for me...you have always respected me. You have never tried to take advantage of me, and you are the only man to this date who has cooked breakfast for me...and that goes back to when we were in college."

"Wow, I didn't know that...Iris, I have to tell you something and I really don't know how." Iris pulled away and said, "Do you have a STD or something?"

"Hell Naw!" Keith retorted. Iris continued, "You're not gay are you?!"

Keith looked at Iris and said, "Come on now...No I'm not gay!"

"Then what is it!?" Iris demanded.

Keith looked at Iris and said quietly, "I'm a virgin..."

Iris looked at Keith in shock. "Quit playing Keith...You're a virgin!" Iris shouted.

"Yes!" Keith admitted.

Then Iris asked, "What about you and Misty Evans?...you all were in the backseat of your car our sophomore year at the drive in..."

"Nothing happened...we kissed and made out a little but...nothing else happened...I have only wanted one woman and I am with her right now...but like I said, I want more than just sex with you...I wanted to marry you back in college and I want to marry you now."

Iris just sat in front of Keith stunned. "I don't know what to say Keith. I don't think I have ever been with a virgin before."

"That was the most difficult thing that I have ever had to confess to anybody." Keith admitted.

Then Iris asked, "So you want to marry me?"

Keith responded, "Iris, I have loved you since we first met. I have dreamed about what our children would look like. I have seen the life that we could live."

"Children?! You mean more than one?"

"Don't you want my children Iris?"

Keith looked at Iris and responded, "See what I'm working with?!"

"Keith, if I am going to get married, I have to get busy with the man that I'm settling down with to see if he can satisfy me..."

Keith turned away for a few seconds, turn back and quietly said, "I will have to see about that." Iris developed a slight grimace to her face and then with the passion of her tigress persona yelled, "What do you mean you will have to see?!"

"Iris, I am going to wait until I get married!" Keith retorted.

Right then Iris went into defense attorney mode, "Alright then, if it's like that, then I want a sexual pre-nuptial agreement!"

Keith looked at Iris with a strange look and then said, "Your kidding right?"

Iris continued, "The agreement will state that if on our wedding night, that we find out that we are not sexually compatible, the marriage will be annulled..."

Keith continued to look at Iris in disbelief and responded, "You're serious?!"

Without blinking, Iris replied, "Serious as a heart attack and a stroke combined!"

Keith thought for a moment and defused the situation by making the remark, "A sexual pre-nupt?...Wow...I guess that could work in both of our favors."

Iris thought of her next move and said, "I can't believe you are a virgin!"

Iris then reached her hand out to Keith. Keith took Iris's hand and looked deeply into her eyes almost seeing her soul and then said, "I love you Iris..."

Hearing the intensity in Keith's voice, a tear ran down Iris's cheek. "Keith, I have been looking for a man to love me the way you have described. I have never let anyone get close enough to my heart to even think about marriage, let alone kids. I have embraced my Iris The Tigress persona, because it kept me strong in those tough lonely times at law school, passing the bar and fighting through the maze of the legal system."

"Sweetness, I love you because you are that strong willed aggressive tigress type woman, but you have to realize that you are getting a strong minded man that is willing to compromise, but will stand up for what he believes in."

Iris looked into Keith's eyes and said, "Kiss me!" Keith just looked at Iris.

Then Iris said, "Please!" Keith reached over and lovingly kissed Iris on her forehead.

Iris smiled and said, "You missed my lips." Keith smiled and replied, "I aimed for what I wanted to kiss."

Iris smiled back and responded, "You are just going to keep teasing me aren't you?"

Then Keith said, "We can always go to city hall." Iris shouted, "You mean right now?!"

Keith smiled, shook his head in the affirmative, but didn't say a word.

Iris thought for a second and said, "Wait here..." Iris walked into her office just on the other side of the kitchen. Keith heard her rambling in there and a few seconds she emerged from her office with a legal pad and a pen. Iris started writing on the pad and presented the note pad to Keith, "Sign it!" Iris commanded.

Keith read over the paper. As he started reading the sheet, he smiled and said, "A sexual pre-nupt?!...you were serious!"

"I have to make sure that you are not a small Jamal!"

Keith looked down at his crotch and said, "I'm not small Jamal..."

In a slightly seductive voice Iris hissed, "Prove It!...I will respect waiting until we say I do, but the

Tigress has to at least see the meat that is going to be served!"

Keith stared at Iris and said, "So what, I'm a piece of meat now?!"

"The only piece of meat that I am concerned with is the one hanging on the lower extremities of your body."

At that point, Keith sensing the sexual tension, began slowly taking off his pants.

Iris watched for a few seconds then said, "That's right nice and slow." Then Iris began rubbing her erect nipples.

Keith watched Iris and as he watched her, he got aroused. Then Keith took off his shirt and was standing in front of Iris totally naked. Then Keith asked, "So what do you think? Is the meat that's served big enough?"

Iris's eyes bulged as she saw his gorgeous body, but without saying a word, Iris took Keith's hand and guided him to sit down. Then she began removing garment after garment off in an almost striptease manner. Keith began to speak and Iris placed a finger over Keith's lips to stop him from speaking. Then she removed her bra and threw it erotically onto Keith's head. Keith smiled and let the bra fall to the floor.

At that point both Keith and Iris were in the kitchen naked as the day they were born. Keith stood up and pull Iris close to him. "Well do you like what you see?" Keith asked.

Iris shook her head in an affirmative manner and responded, "Do you?" Keith smiled and shook his head in an affirmative manner.

Then Iris inquired, "So what do we do now?" Keith said one word, "Kiss!"

Iris jumped into Keith's arms and wrapped her legs around his waist like a python. Keith picked Iris up and placed her on top of the marble countertop of the island. They began kissing and Iris ran her hand along Keith's back and slowly moved her hands to his chest and Keith began kissing Iris's neck and earlobes.

Iris took her slender fingers and grabbed a hold of Keith's manhood and put it right to the pearly gates, but she did not insert it. She just let Keith feel the warmth and wetness, then whispered, "Are you sure you want to wait? Doesn't that feel good baby?"

Keith whispered back, "It will feel even better when we say, I Do...this is the compromise." And pulled away. Iris snapped her fingers and said, "Damn! I almost had it!...I should have just put it in..."

Keith smiled and said, "I should have let you...But you didn't!" and began to laugh.

Iris smiled and began laughing herself and said, "We still can!"

Keith slowly stopped laughing and remark, "After we get back from city hall, we can pick up from where we stopped."

Iris smiled and said, "Compromise..." Then she kissed Keith once more on the cheek and said, "Let me go get dressed, it's my wedding day."

Keith said, Yeah, I better get dressed, it is my wedding day too and I am the luckiest man in the world."

Then Iris remarked, I am the luckiest woman. I've got the man that I have always wanted and the tiger who is man enough to stand up to the tigress."

Then Keith questioned, "A black tiger and tigress, that is a rare species. What is the world going to do with us?"

Iris thought for a second and said, "Bow down to us because the world is ours!" and with that they shared one last kiss and walked into what would be a beautiful future together.

EIGHT

DESSERT BY BLINDFOLD

*N*atasha was a single independent attractive woman. She had long black straight hair with a smooth medium brown skin tone and a nicely curved frame, along with a warm inviting smile and very bubbly personality.

Even with all of that, she was going through a transitional period in life. She was working part time as a medical clerk in a small community hospital and was in school full time in order to finish her master's degree. She did not know what she wanted to do after school was completed.

She would ask several people at her job for advice and no one could offer her any insight to future possibilities in regard to her career path. Her supervisor Stacy was a real asshole of a person and would go out of her way to discourage Natasha from attaining any higher aspirations and personal goals because Stacy didn't have a college degree herself and was fearful that Natasha with her youth and likeability would one day take her job.

Stacy would schedule Natasha to work on days that Stacy knew Natasha had major exams and then would tell Natasha, "Oh, I forgot that you were in school..." or "We did not have anyone else to work your shift..."

One day as Natasha was at work filing medical report, a new face appeared on the unit. He was stocky in stature and stood about 5' 9" and weighed about 215 lbs. He looked like he could have been a good running back based on his size. He had a bronze brown skin tone with a five o'clock shadow. His hair was neatly cut with an intricate style designed on the right side.

As he approached Natasha, Natasha looked up from filing, smiled and said, "May I help you?"

The gentleman responded, "Yes, I am Dr. Allen Ramsey, I am the new resident here and I think I am lost."

Natasha asked, "Where are you trying to go?" Allen answered, "2 northwest?"

"Ok...well you are not too far off course...You just go down the hall make a right, walk about half the corridor and make another right walk until you get to a set of doors make a left and...you know what...let me just show you...by the way, I'm Natasha."

Allen smiled and said, "I would really appreciate that Natasha..." Natasha smiled and walked out from behind the counter.

As she walked passed Allen, he noticed that she had the scent of spicy cinnamon and remarked, "Please don't get offended and this is not a come on line, but when you walked passed me, I closed my eyes and thought of eating apple pie..."

Natasha stopped turn and looked at Allen and said, "That really did sound like a come on line, but it's cool and I'm not offended." She smiled, turned around and began walking.

Allen slowly followed behind her noticing the way her body moved to and fro as she walked and as he followed Natasha said, "Don't be back there looking at my goodies!"

Allen sped up his pace and said, "I wasn't doing that..." and started chuckling.

Natasha smiled and responding, "Umm Hmm..." As they walked Natasha asked, "So where are you from?"

"I am from the mid-west...where are you from?" "Right here...a home-grown product."

"Ok...well I am new in town, I have only been here for two weeks and I really hate eating alone... if you are not busy this evening, would you like to get something to eat? Maybe you could show me what's good and what I should avoid in this town."

Natasha stopped walking and looked at Allen then said, "I don't date co-workers..."

Allen said, "Ok, I can respect that...but technically we don't work together. I will be working at 2 northwest and you work back there wherever that was...let's look at it as to colleagues having a meal and getting to know one another."

Natasha smiled and said, "That was smooth...ok...call me... here is my number." Natasha went into her pocket, pulled out a notepad and wrote her number on the sheet and handed to Allen.

Allen looked at the number then went into his wallet and handed Natasha his business card and said, "Here is my number...It has to be an even exchange amongst colleagues." Natasha began walking again. Allen stood there for a few seconds watching as Natasha walked and Natasha said, "There you go again looking at my goodies..." and began giggling.

Allen started walking to catch up. As they walked down the corridors, Allen inquired, "What is it like working around here?"

"I will tell you tonight when we are having something to eat...the walls have ears..."

"Ok, I understand." They made their last turn and Natasha said, "Well, here we are 2 northwest."

"Thank you so much...I appreciated you going out of your way to make sure I made it to my unit."

Natasha smiled and said, "It was no problem...I am looking forward to dinner...amongst colleagues." and smiled.

Allen thought for a moment and said, "Why don't we just leave after work? I will be done at 5:00PM. I know I will be hungry then."

Natasha thought for a second and said, "You know that would work...I know a little spot that has happy hour specials and tonight they have an open mic...I really like spoken work."

"Oh really, I write a little poetry...I might get up and bless the mic."

"Oh you know the lingo so you must have done your fair share of open mics."

"You will see or rather hear this evening...while two colleagues enjoy a meal together." Natasha looked at Allen smiled and turned to walk *back to her unit. As she was walking Allen continued to watch Natasha. As she walked she purposefully added a little more switch in her hips and in a louder voice but less than a yell shouted, "Doc! Stop staring at my goodies...I see you in the mirror!" and giggled.*

Allen stated, "Your goodies are so good to look at!"

As Natasha walked back to her unit, she began thinking about if she was making a mistaking going out with Allen. She thought he was an attractive man, better still a doctor and she felt a chemistry between them, but she remembered listening to her friends that got into relationship at the job and they ended horribly.

All Natasha kept hearing in her mind was something her friends would say, "Girl, don't get your meat and your bread at the same place!" Then Natasha would try to convince herself that this was not a date. To herself she would say, "It's just two colleagues having a meal and listening to some poetry together..." Then in the next minute she would say to herself, "Who am I kidding, this is a date..."

As the time got closer to time to get off Natasha was filled with anticipation. She could hardly concentrate. At 4:45, Natasha's supervisor Stacy came out of her office and said to Natasha, "I need you to stay over and help with the inventory of the supplies."

Natasha looked at Stacy with a bit of resentment and responded, "I can't tonight...I have plans..." Stacy looked and said, "Your date with the new doctor will have to wait, you are needed here!"

Natasha stared at Stacy and replied, "I don't know what you are talking about, but I am not staying over and that is that!"

Stacy stared back at Natasha and said, "If you want to keep your job, you will cancel your plans and do this inventory..."

Natasha thought for a second and then yelled out , "Did you just threaten me?!...I heard a threat...we can take this up with human resources!"

Stacy looked around and saw all the witnesses who heard the exchange of words and replied, "I didn't threaten you..."

Natasha continued, "I heard you threaten that if I didn't do what you wanted me to do that I would lose my job...that is a threat and I don't take kindly to threats..."

Stacy said, "It was not a threat, we just need this done and it is in your job description."

Then Natasha answered, "But you wait until the end of the day to bring this to me...the supplies will be there tomorrow, and I will do inventory on them then...otherwise, I am more than willing to take this up with Human Resources."

Knowing that she had already had grievances filed against her in the recent past Stacy just turned away and said, "Just get it done by tomorrow..."

Natasha gathered her belongings and walked out from behind the counter. She walked to the door and said to herself, "I hate bullshit!"

When the sun hit her face, she felt like a weight had been lifted off of her shoulders. She got into her car, took a deep breath and pulled out her cell phone. She took out Allen's business card and dialed the number. After the first ring Allen answered, "Dr. Ramsey speaking..."

"Hello Dr. Ramsey speaking..." "Well hello, is this the Goodie monster?"

"I should be calling you the Goodie monster, the way you be looking at my goodies..."and they both started laughing.

"So where are we going to eat?" Allen asked. "After the day that I've had, can we get a drink?"

Natasha responded. "Sure...I would love a drink...do you have a place in mind?" "I sure do, as a matter of fact, tonight is spoken word night."

"Really?!...I know my way around a mic..." "You have lyrical skills?!"

"Don't let the smooth look fool you..."

Ok Doc...we will see...the place is at 1251 W. Taylor."

"I know where that is...okay I will see you in about 20 minutes."

"Ok see you then, I can't wait to see your skills on the mic." "Ok see you soon."

"Ok bye."

As Natasha got off of the phone, she had a sense of feeling rejuvenated. Her feelings of anticipation were in overdrive. Every stoplight felt like it was lasting an hour. Traffic seemed to be much longer than it was. Finally, she had arrived at the spot of the night festivities.

Natasha took a quick look in the mirror of her car to make sure she looked presentable. She looked in her purse and took out some Chap Stick. She applied the Chap Stick to her lips and said to herself, "Even though this isn't a date, I can't have dry crusty lips."

She smiled at herself in the mirror and then exited the car. As she walked towards the door of the club, she noticed a midnight blue Maserati sports car pull into the parking lot and park.

As she continued to walk towards the door and Natasha heard a voice ring out, "Is that the Goodie Monster I see?"

A big smile came onto Natasha's face and Natasha yelled back, "Hey You!"

Natasha waited will Allen caught up to her. "I feel really hyped!" Allen said enthusiastically.

"Ok...I hope you're ready..." Natasha said as Allen opened the door for her. As they walked through the door, the place was a little over halfway full.

Natasha stated, "It's gonna be a full house tonight..."

They walked towards the middle of the club and to their left they found a table for two. As they walked over to the table, Allen pulled out the chair for Natasha.

Natasha looked at Allen and said, "A man with manners, I like that."

"Well, I was raised by my momma and my daddy. My mom believed in manners and education, my dad, work ethic and money. They both believed in discipline. You put the sum of the two together and you get the product which is me." Allen responded.

"Ok!..." Natasha said.

Then Allen asked, "Do you ever get on the mic?"

"Never!" Natasha answered.

"Why?" Allen inquired.

"I hear some of these people get up on stage and are really good...then I hear the really bad ones and I have the feelings that I just don't want to get embarrassed." Natasha answered.

"I understand being afraid on stage, but for me. I haven't been booed yet..." Allen stated.

Just then the waitress walked over and asked, "Will you be having anything this evening?"

Allen looked at Natasha and asked the waitress, "Are there any specials this evening?"

"Drink specials or dinner specials?" The waitress questioned.

Natasha stated, "I didn't know you all served food here..." Then she turn to Allen and said, "Doc...do you want to just eat here? Because after the show, trying to find a place that may be open is going to be difficult....we can kill two birds with one stone by eating here."

Allen thought for a second and said, "That's cool with me Goodie..." and smiled.

Natasha looked at Allen with a pleasingly surprised look on her face and then said,

"Goodie?!...so is that what you're gonna call me from now on?"

Allen continued smiling and said, "If you don't mind..."

Natasha looked alluringly into Allen's eyes and said, "No... I don't mind, but that stays between us Doc."

Allen looked back into Natasha's eyes and said, "Or I could call you bugs' bunny, the way you be calling me Doc." And they both began to laugh.

And Natasha replied, "You've got jokes. I love a man with a sense of humor...DOC!"

Then the waitress cut in, "Well, we have a hot wing special...20 wings and fries for $10. As for the drinks, we have beers on tap for $0.75...they come in a 4oz cup and then we have 8oz Long Island Ice Tea for $2.50."

"Are the Long Islands strong?" Natasha asked.

The waitress said, "They are nice...they can lay you down if you're not careful!"

"I will have one...Doc how about you?" "I think I will have a Tito's and cranberry...do you want to get the wings?"

"Sure!"

"Ok, we are going to have one Long Island, one Tito's with cranberry and the wings special."

The waitress took the order and walked away. Just then the lights dimmed, and smooth jazz started to play in the background.

All of a sudden, a voice echoed out, "Welcome to The Hot Spot...tonight is Words for the World. This is our weekly open mic and if you so wish you can sign up to sing, tell jokes or my favorite...express yourself with some spoken word. We will be getting started in a few minutes. If there is anyone that wants to get on the mic, please see me and get signed up...By the way I am YTILAER, your host for this evening's festivities."

Right then, Allen got up and walked over to where the sign sheet was. As he got over to the sign sheet, he looked in Natasha's direction and she was looking in his direction. Allen signed in and came back over to where they were seated.

Natasha looked at Allen as he approached and said, "Soooo...You are really gonna get on the mic tonight huh Doc?"

Allen looked at Natasha and said, "I ain't never scared...besides, I have a special piece for you."

"OH REALLY!!!" Natasha exclaimed. Just then, the waitress brought their drinks.

"*Your wings will be here shortly.*" The waitress stated. Then she walked away. Just then, the host YTILAER broadcasted, "We are getting it started, right here right now. We have a few rules, not many, but a few...first and foremost, respect the mic.

We don't mind you conversing, but keep it just above a whisper, next rule, show everyone respect...You may not agree with what is being said, but it takes a lot to come up here and share a piece of your soul with the crowd. Third rule, respect yourself...if you are drinking, stay this side of fucked up...don't be the one that security drags up out of here...with that being said, let's get it started... We have a thick list tonight...and since the list is so thick, we asks that you do one piece that is five minutes or less...this list tells me that it will be a good night tonight...we have a bunch of virgins that we have to break in tonight, but we are gonna take it nice and slow...so let's do this...coming to the mic...a virgin to our mic...he calls himself...Doctor Love...lets show some love for Doctor Love."

The crowd began to clap and at that point Allen got up nervously and began walking toward the microphone. As Allen got in front of the microphone, the crowd could tell he was not used to being in front of crowds.

Then Allen spoke, "Hello..." The crowd in unison yelled, "Hello!" Allen continued, "This piece is for a special someone... I think back to when we first met...since then I can't stop thinking of her beauty.

She has the whole package and to observe her is purely magic. She just leaves you... mystified. Every aspect of her is tantalizing. I crave her touch. Her smile is as bright as the halo of an angel. Her eyes pierce you like daggers. Her mind is as sharp as a razor's edge.

Her body can easily be mistaken for that of a goddess. She moves like a stalking panther, slow and precise calculating every step. She could keep the rhythm of a drum in perfect beat. Her voice is like the sound of wind chimes caught on the breeze of a warm clear summer day.

She speaks just above a whisper. But like a gong her voice reverberates over and over in the recesses of my mind. In a daydream or maybe it was a fantasy, I approached her and said, "May I hold your hands and look into your eyes?"

"Can we encounter the depths of each other's soul?"

The sun and moon do not compare to you in beauty. Desire is a fire that burns forever in your essences. I see your hands reaching for stars and touching galaxies that are not within reach, yet you grasp them effortlessly. You will know when you have touched my heart because that was when we first met...On our special day..."

Then Allen paused for a second and looked into the crowd. At that point, someone in the crowd yelled out, "All right now!" And the crowd started to clap. Then before Allen left the mic while the crowd was still clapping, Allen said on the mic, "That piece was for the Goodie Monster, but from now on I will just call her Goodie, because she is too fine to be anybody's monster."

Then Allen walked back to his seat. Shocked Natasha was smiling and blushing at the same time. Then Allen said, well what did you think?"

Speechless, all Natasha could say was "WOW!"

"So did you like the piece?"

"Yes I did...you really have lyrical skills!"

"I don't want to brag, but..."and Allen began to laugh.

"Modest too..."Natasha replied.

At this point, dinner came and they enjoyed their meal.

As they were eating, Allen asked, "So how was your day?"

"It was not great...my manager is a real piece of work."

"Your manager is Stacy right?"

"Yes...that heifer tried to stop me from going out tonight!"

"How?" Allen inquired.

"You know what? let's not ruin our beautiful night talking about her."

"Ok, that's cool with me...so what else would you like to do tonight?...considering that this is not a date."

"Well, I would like some dessert."

"Ok, what do you have a taste for?"

Natasha thought for a second and said, "Surprise me."

Allen responded, "I have some sweets at my place, but I don't want you to feel uncomfortable coming to my place."

Natasha reiterated, "Like you said, what is wrong with to colleagues having dessert after a meal."

"Ok, well you can follow me or I can drive and then bring you back to your car...it's your choice."

"I don't mind riding with you."

Then with a big Cheshire cat grin Allen asked Natasha, "Hey, do you want to pull a dine and dash?"

Natasha cracked a smile and said in a whisper, "Are you serious?"

Allen gave a sneaky look and then replied, "Naw, I just wanted to see how adventurous you are."

Natasha giggled and got out of her seat. Allen walk to the counter and paid the bill. As he was paying, he watched Natasha walk towards the door. Allen got his change and slowly walked behind Natasha.

"Are you still trying to look at my goodies?" Natasha asked and giggled.

Allen smiled and sped up his pace in order to open the door for Natasha."

As Natasha walked through the door and towards Allen's car, she noticed a blind man with a cane. Allen opened the car door and Natasha got into the car. Allen closed the door behind her and walked around to the other side. When he got to the other side, his door was already opened by Natasha.

Allen got in the car and said, "Why thank you Goodie!" and laughed.

Natasha responded, "That's the least I could do." Allen started the car and proceeded to leave the parking lot.

Natasha again noticed the blind man walking and posed a question. "Doc, is it true that if a person loses one of their senses, the other senses become stronger?" "Honestly, I don't know...I have read studies that suggest that the other senses do become more enhanced...but other studies have suggested the opposite. It may depend on the sense that is lost...but that is according to the reports...I have heard that the sense of touch and hearing are more acute in the blind and spatial and visual acuity is improved in the deaf, but I really don't know.

Now if you want to test the theory, we can." Natasha smiled and asked, "How can we do that Doc?"

"Well, we are going to be having dessert, lets test if our senses get stronger if one of is taken away."

"For real, are you serious?" Natasha questioned.

"If you are up too it I am!" Allen stated.

"OK!" Natasha enthusiastically confirmed as they pulled up to Allen's apartment. Natasha began to wonder what Allen had for dessert.

Allen parked and got out of the car. He went to open the car door for Natasha, and she was already out of the car. Allen stopped in his tracks and said, "I was going to get that for you."

Natasha replied, "I know, but I am ready for dessert and our little experiment."

"Alright, Enthusiasm!

I like that! Are you this enthusiastic about everything you do?"

Natasha said in a seductive manner, "Only in things that I enjoy doing..."

Allen paused for a couple of seconds and then walked to his apartment door. Allen allowed Natasha to walk into the apartment first. Natasha noticed that the living room was designed in a chic modern design. It looked as if an interior decorator had designed the place. The living room was white, black, glass and chrome. The couch was black Italian leather. The coffee table was glass and chrome and the fireplace was white marble.

"Nice place..." Natasha commented.

"Thank you." Allen replied.

Allen invited Natasha to have a seat as he picked up the remote control. Allen pushed a button and the fireplace flamed up. He pushed another button and Dave Brubeck's Take Five began to play. Natasha sat and didn't say a word. Allen walked into the kitchen and Natasha heard rumbling, rattling and the clinking of glass.

Then Allen asked, "Can we start the experiment with the absence of the sense of sight?"

Natasha paused for a second and then answered, "Sure, why not?"

Allen came out of the kitchen and went into another room that was down the hallway. A few seconds later, he came back to the living room with a black satin scarf. Then he asked, "Are you sure this is not a date?" and smiled.

Natasha smiled back at Allen and responded, "No dammit, this is not a date!" and started laughing.

Allen laughed along with her and said, "OK...I have this satin scarf. This can make a good blindfold."

Natasha looked at the scarf, then took it out of Allen's hand and rubbed it across her face. She felt how smooth it felt and then said anxiously, "Ok, blindfold me!"

Allen paused for a second and asked nervously, "Are you sure you want to do this?"

"Yes Doc, come on, hurry up! I trust you."

Apprehensive, Allen said, "Ok...Ok!"

In an aggressive manner she stated, "And make it tight!"

"Have you done this before?" Allen said sarcastically. Natasha answered in a similar sarcastic voice, "No...I have not been blindfolded, may have been tied up, but not blindfolded." Then Natasha laughed.

Allen paused again and said, "Oh really?!" "That was a joke Doc!" Natasha continued laughing. As Allen put the blindfold over Natasha's eyes, he began to feel slightly uneasy.

"Tighter!" Natasha exclaimed.

Allen made the blindfold tighter and said, "How is that?"

"That's good right there."

Allen walked back into the kitchen and brought out a tray of different desserts.

Then Allen said, "Ok, I have a few things that you might or might not like...but first, are you allergic to anything?"

"No!"

"Ok...open your mouth."

Natasha paused and then shouted, "Don't put nothing nasty in my mouth!"

Allen walked over to Natasha and placed his crotch close to her ear and pulled down the zipper. Hearing the zipper go down, Natasha calmly, but seriously said, "Don't Play!"

Allen chuckled, and said, "I guess hearing does improve when you lose your sight."

Then Allen zipped up his pants and said, "Open your mouth and stick out your tongue!" Natasha stuck out her tongue and began flickering it like a snake. Allen took a piece of red velvet cake and placed it on Natasha's tongue. She took the piece of cake in and began savoring the multitudes of flavors that were present in her mouth.

"That is good!" said Natasha.

"Can you tell me what it is?"

"Well, I know it's cake."

"What kind?"

"The cake has so many flavors, but if I would have to guess, I would have to say Red Velvet...Am I right?"

"I will let you know at the end of the experiment."

Natasha let out a sigh and said, "Ok!"

Then Allen barely touched the side of Natasha's cheek with a spoon and asked, "Did you feel that?"

Natasha replied, "Barely..."

Allen took the spoon and dipped it into some chocolate ice cream and said, "What is this?"

Natasha opened her mouth and Allen placed the spoonful of ice cream in her mouth. Without hesitation Natasha yelled, "That's chocolate ice cream!" Without responding Allen took some of icing from the red velvet cake and spread it all over a slice of strawberry and said, "Ok, what is this?"

Natasha opened her mouth and Allen placed the sour cream icing covered strawberry slice onto her tongue. Natasha tasted the strawberry and said, "That is different...I taste the strawberry, but I can't make out the other flavor."

Then Allen said, "Ok, if this is going to be a true experiment, I will need to be the other subject. I have set up another tray, I will bring it out and then I will be blindfolded, and you give me a dessert and we will see if there is a difference in the senses."

Allen went to the kitchen and brought out the second tray. Allen took off Natasha's blindfold and placed it over his eyes. Natasha stood up and went behind Allen and tightened the scarf over Allen's eyes.

Then Natasha said, "Now Doc, stick out your tongue and say Aaahhh..." Allen started to laugh, and then he stuck out his tongue and said, "Aaahhh!" Natasha took a piece of the piece of cake and placed some ice cream on top of the cake and put the combination of ice cream and cake on the tip of Allen's tongue.

Allen tasted the cake and ice cream and said, "That is good, but I forgot, I know everything on the trays, so I have a better chance at guessing them."

Natasha thought for a second, then said, "I have an idea! I am going to get something out of the refrigerator and even though you know what is on the trays, you won't know what I have added. Then it will be a truly blind experiment."

Allen said, "Ok, the kitchen is to your left." Natasha walked from the couch and acted like she was walking to the kitchen, but she just took a few steps waited a few seconds and then said, "Ok, I'm back."

Natasha took some ice cream and placed it on the tip of the spoon and said, "Doc...stick out your tongue and tell me what the flavor is..." Allen stuck out his tongue and Natasha placed the ice cream on her tongue and then placed her tongue with the ice cream onto Allen's tongue. She then pushed Allen back on the couch and straddled him. They began to French kiss.

After about 30 seconds of kissing, Allen broke the kiss and said, "That tasted like Goodie Monster covered in chocolate ice cream!"

Natasha laughed and responded, "You are correct!" Allen pulled the blindfold off and asked, "So, are we going to finally consider this a first date?"

Natasha slowly stopped laughing. She looked warmly and passionately into Allen's eyes and answered, "Yes Doc...this is our first date."

Allen smiled, looked into Natasha eyes, gently stroked her right cheek with his index finger and leaned towards Natasha. Natasha leaned closer to Allen and they kissed again and enjoyed kissing each other for the rest of their night together.

NINE

FORBIDDEN FRUIT

*S*kylar Livingston was a single, very attractive, shy, introverted, logistical analysist that worked for an up and coming computer Software Company.

Joshua Danton was a very handsome executive director in the company. He was very outgoing and has it all, a beautiful super model wife with two remarkable children, a big pretty house on the hill along with nice cars and all of the other toys that can be equated with success.

One day, Skylar notice discrepancies in some of the accounting numbers for the upcoming mergers with another software company. Skylar would hear all of the other female coworkers talk about how fine Joshua was and how they would flirt with him and that he would never respond because he was so committed to his family.

Harriet was Joshua's secretary and she was the company gossip. When Skylar approached Joshua's office, Harriet was gathering her things to take her coffee break.

Harriet stated, "Girl, are you going in to see Mr. Danton?

I wish I was you...I would love to get his fine ass all alone...I would put it on him." Then Harriet started laughing.

Skylar didn't respond to Harriet's comment and walked up to Joshua's office door. Skylar was nervous and didn't know what reaction to expect when she presented the information that she had gathered.

Skylar knocked on the door. In a very masculine voice she heard, "Come In." When Skylar walked through the door, her heart almost skipped a beat. She looked at Joshua and, in her mind, she thought, "Damn! He does look good!"

Joshua was wearing a black pinned stripped double-breasted Tom Ford suit. On his feet were black polished ostrich skinned Tom Ford shoes and a rose gold and diamond Cartier watch was on his wrist. Joshua had a nice neat haircut and was cleanly shaved. Joshua was looking out of the window as Skylar enter the office. When Joshua turned around, his heart dropped into his stomach when he noticed Skylar. She was wearing a purple, white and black shear fitted dress. Her black wavy hair was in a French roll. Joshua was intrigued at the fact that even though Skylar was wearing no make-up, she had a radiant beauty that made her almost glow.

"You must be Skylar? I have heard good things about you." Joshua announced.

"Yes sir." Skylar replied in a shy intimidated voice.

"Please, don't call me sir. That makes me feel like an old man..." and Joshua smiled.

Skylar responded, "Ok...Mr. Danton."
"No...Mr. Danton makes me feel like my father....just call me Joshua."

"Ok Joshua..."

"So where do we stand on the case of the merger." Joshua asked.

"Well, all of the calculations are completed except for this section here. I have completed all of the other necessary paperwork. I need you to make sure these discrepancies are accounted for. Once you do that then all that will be needed is your signature."

Joshua looked over the paperwork. As he looked at the papers, Skylar could not take her eyes off of Joshua.

"Ok, I see the problem, but those discrepancies were addressed in the addendum." Joshua said. Joshua signed off on the paperwork and said, "Now that that is done, I can go to the photo shoot for the promotional."

Skylar looked over Joshua's attire and noticed that his tie was crooked and his handkerchief was off center. Then Skylar said, "Well you might want to straighten your tie if you are participating in a photo shoot."

Joshua attempted to adjust his tie, but he realized that he didn't have a mirror and asked, "Would you fix it for me? I don't have a mirror in here and I am really not the suit and tie type."

Skylar nervously approached Joshua and said, "Sure, I will fix it." As she reached up to adjust the tie, she looked into Joshua grey green eyes and a feeling came over her that she had never experienced before. Her heart started racing and her hands began to shake. As Joshua looked back into Skylar's golden hazel eyes, he began having knots in his stomach.

As Skylar finished adjusting his tie and handkerchief, with a slight bit of uneasiness Joshua said, "Thank you for the adjustment."

"I just want you to make a good impression...for the company."

"I am going to try my best to make THE COMPANY look good." Joshua smiled while looking into Skylar's eyes for about seven seconds then he broke the gaze and walked passed Skylar.

Skylar looked towards Joshua's desk and saw the picture of Joshua's family on the window sill. She turned and followed behind Joshua to leave out of his office. As they walked down the hall, towards the elevator Skylar said, "You have a lovely Family."

Joshua smiled and said, "I am truly blessed." Joshua pushed the button for the elevator and as Skylar and Joshua waited at the elevator, Harriet walked by the two of them, smiled and winked at them both. As Harriet passed by, Skylar and Joshua looked at each other and laughed as they were getting onto the elevator.

"What was that all about?" Joshua asked.

Skylar responded, "You tell me..." Joshua allowed Skylar to get on the elevator first, he noticed the shapely definition of her body and once they got onto the elevator, Joshua truly paid attention to the fragrance of Skylar's perfume and the scent was intoxicating. Skylar pushed the button for the 1st floor and the doors closed.

As the elevator started moving, Joshua commented, "You really smell good...what are you wearing?"

Skylar smiled and bashfully said, "A Savage's Pheromone..."

Joshua replied, "It has the perfect name...it definitely can bring out the savage beast in a man ..."and Joshua chuckled.

"Oh really!" Skylar commented with her continued smile.

Before Joshua could respond, the elevator made a loud screeching noise and then the elevator stopped. Skylar let out a high pitch screamed and then yelled out, "What the hell was that?!"

Worried but keeping a brave face, Joshua calmly said, "I don't know, but I don't like it..." Joshua pushed the buttons in the elevator and then opened the console that housed the emergency telephone in the elevator. There was no dial tone on the emergency telephone.

"The phone is dead..." Joshua said.

Skylar began to shake and then she began to pace two or three steps back and forth. "I don't like being in confining places..." Skylar nervously said.

A few minutes seemed like hours to Skylar. As more time passed, Skylar was more and more terrified. She started pacing more and more and finally she broke down and had an all-out panic attack. She screamed out, "I've got to get out of here!" and she began hysterically crying.

Joshua took Skylar's hands and said, "Hey, it's going to be ok...I've got you...we will be fine."

Then he looked into her eyes. As he looked into her eyes, he noticed the tears streaming down her cheeks. Joshua cupped her face with his hands. With his thumbs, he wiped the tears off of her cheeks. Then he put his arms around Skylar and said, "I am not going to let anything happen to you...we are in this together."

Skylar placed her head onto Joshua's chest. She took solace when she heard the calm rhythm of Joshua's heartbeat. Joshua, while holding Skylar in his arms, smelled Skylar's perfume again and it made him sexually aroused. Joshua began to have an erection that Skylar felt. Skylar put her arms around Joshua's lower back and pulled him closer to her so that she could fully feel his hardness. The two were caught up in the sexual tension that they were experiencing and at that point nothing mattered but the embraced that they shared.

As they continue to embrace, they did not realize that the elevator began moving. Skylar began rubbing on Joshua's upper and lower back and then began rubbing the upper portion of his buttocks. Joshua ran his hands along Skylar's slender frame and his hands rested just above her butt cheeks.

Joshua heard the ding of the elevator and realized that the elevator was at the first floor. Joshua pulled slightly away, and Skylar continued to hold on to Joshua. Joshua said, "We are on the ground lever... the doors are about to open..."

Skylar looked up at Joshua, kissed him on the lips and said, "Thank you so much for being there for me..."

Joshua pulled away a little more but very slowly. Then he stopped pulling away altogether and said in a gasp, "No problem..." Then Joshua looked at Skylar, he slow moved closer to Skylar and kissed her on the forehead and said, "I told you we would be ok..."

At that instant, the doors open and a number of co-workers were standing in front of the elevator.

The coworkers asked, "Are you ok?" Both Joshua and Skylar said, "We are ok..."

As they walked out of the elevator, Joshua went to the right and Skylar went to the left. Joshua looked back at Skylar and Skylar looked back at Joshua.

Then Joshua said, "See you later MS Livingston."

Skylar smiled and said, "See you soon Mr. Danton..." and they walked their separate ways thinking about a future together that they may someday share.

TEN

THE SCAVENGER HUNT

Maya had longed for a birthday celebration. While growing up, she would see friends and other relatives have birthday parties and they would get gifts. Maya never did because of her parents' religious beliefs.

Justin was a close friend to Maya. He had known her for years and there had always been sexual tension and chemistry between them, but neither wanted to compromise their friendship. The two would talk on a daily basis. They would talk about everything. Justin thought about giving Maya a birthday gift that she would remember forever. A day before Maya's 30th birthday Justin called Maya as he had done many times before, however this conversation would bring a change to their relationship.

"Hello, beautiful!" Justin said as Maya answered her phone.

"Well hello you!" Maya responded.

"If you could have anything for your birthday, what would you want?"

"Honestly, I don't know..."

"Come on...you have to want something..."

"Ok, if I could have anything, I would want a birthday that I would never forget..."

Justin thought for a few seconds then he said, "Ok...I have something planned that I think you will never forget."

"Oh really!? What do you have planned?"

"Tomorrow, you will have a birthday that you have always wanted. However, there will be some rules that you will need to follow."

"Rules? What are you cooking up?"

"Well, let's just say that you will get the birthday you have always wanted, but you will have to agree to follow the rules...will you follow the rules?"

Maya thought for a second. Intrigued she said, "OK!"

Justin then said, "Rule number 1, we cannot communicate with each other until the end of the day. Rule number 2, the only text that can be sent is *thumbs up or thumbs down emoji if you like or dislike what has been given to you for your birthday at that particular interval of the day. Rule number 3, you must follow the clues that will take you to your next set of clues that will, in the end, give you your big surprise. Do you think you can handle that?"*

Maya thought for a few seconds and replied, "Sure!"

"Ok, starting after we get off of the phone, the rules will begin. Your first clue is...you like it hot, dark and strong everyday...make sure you go to where you get it on the regular...see you tomorrow beautiful."

Then Justin hung up the phone. Right then Maya knew exactly where to go. Throughout the night Maya wondered what her birthday was going to be like. As she got in bed to get some sleep, she got more and more restless. As she finally fell asleep, she continued tossing and turning. At 6:00 am, her alarm woke her, and she went through her usual morning routine. By 7:00am, Maya walked to her car and there was an envelope under her windshield wiper blade. Maya looked around, but she didn't see anyone. She took the envelope off of the windshield and opened it. Inside was a card and a gift card. The only thing the card said was the clue that she had received from Justin the night before. The gift card was from Pure Elegance Beauty Salon and Spa. Maya smiled and got into her car. She started the car, but before she put the car in gear, she sent Justin the thumbs up emoji.

Maya put the car in gear and proceed to the Starbucks that she goes to every morning. When she arrived, she walked through the door and went to the counter.

"Happy Birthday Maya!" said the Starbucks manager. Shocked, Maya said, "Why thank you!" Then the manager handed Maya a Chocolate Chia Tea latte and a card.

Maya looked at the card and said, "What is this?" The manager smiled and said, "It's your next clue and the drink is compliments of Starbuck for your birthday. Maya smiled and said, "Thank you so much."

She immediately texted Justin and sent another thumbs up emoji. Then she read the next clue and it said, "Go to the place where you have your do done...hint...the gift will tell the tell...reservations are at Nine." Maya thought for a minute then looked at the gift card and said to herself, "I know where this is." Then Maya, got in her car and began driving.

As she started to drive, all kinds of questions came in her mind. Then she thought to herself, "Justin has put a lot of thought in this I wonder how long this plan has been in place?" As Maya pulled up to the hair salon, she noticed familiar faces standing outside of the salon. Maya parked the car and got out. To her surprise, standing out front were three of her best friends that she had not seen in years, Shondra, Josie and Monica.

"Hey Girl! Happy Birthday!" the three said in unison.

"What the hell?!" Maya exclaimed. Maya continued, "How did you know I would be here?"

Shondra responded, "A sexy fine big birdie told me and I shared with the girls..." And they started laughing.

Then Josie said, "C'mon in here so we can catch up and get our hair did and body done." The door opened and the stylist Jasmine smiled and said, "Hey birthday girl...we have a special treatment for you today.

Maya paused for a second and then said, "What special treatment?" Just then there was a loud POP.

Josie yelled out, "Mimosas Baby!" Then Shondra pull out a flask and said, "Hell Naw, this is your 30th birthday, we are having Champagne Screws...who knows, the champagne screw might get you screwed!" and they all started laughing.

Then Maya said, "If only I had someone to screw..." Josie remarked, It has to be someone that you are getting down and dirty with!"

Maya just smiled, looked to the floor and said, "Nope!"

Monica stated, "We are going to change all of that!" After all of the drinks were poured, Monica said, "A toast to my girl for her 30th...we love you..." Everyone yelled, "Cheers!" and took a drink.

Then they sat in the chairs and let the stylist do their things. As they talked, caught up and were pampered with massages, Jasmine handed Maya an envelope. Maya opened the envelope and the card read, "Now that your do is did and you are feeling right, hopefully your head is not too tight, ask your girls for the box!"

Curious, Maya said, "I am supposed to ask you guys for the box?"

The three friends looked at each other and said in unison, "What box?" and began laughing.

Then Josie said, "Do you mean this box and brought out of a closet a long box that had Neiman

Marcus engraved in gold on the top of it. Then, Monica yelled, "Open it!"

Maya took the box and apprehensively opened the box. When she looked inside of it, a rush of adrenalin overcame her.

Shondra yelled, "What's in the box Girl?" Maya slowly reached into the box and pulled out a black and gold sequence gown. Also in the box was a pair matching black and gold Stiletto shoes and another envelope.

Shondra picked up the envelope and handed it to Maya. Maya took out the next clue. The card read, "I hope you are enjoying your day, but it's nothing compared to what your night will be like...Take yourself to heaven on earth. When you get there see the concierge for your next gift."

Maya thought for a few seconds and said, "Oh no he didn't!" Then she broke into a big smile.

Her girlfriends started yelling, "What did he do girl?"

Maya smiled and said, "That's personal!" "Maya, you can't keep that from us, we are your girls!"

Maya responded, "I will call you all tomorrow."

Just then Josie said, "That smile on your face says that we may not hear from you in another few years."

Maya hugged her friends and thanked them for the spa treatment. Then Maya picked up the box and went out to her car. Before she started it, she sent Justin a double thumbs up emoji. Maya drove to the Essence of the Empress Casino and Resort. This was one of those bucket list type of resorts. Stars and celebrities at times had difficulty getting reservations here. Maya pulled up and the doorman opened her car door.

"Welcome to the Essence of the Empress, I hope you enjoy your stay."

Maya stated, "I am sure I will...can you tell me were the concierge is?"

The doorman answered, "Right around that corner to your right."

"Thank you." Maya replied. Maya followed the directions. Once she got the concierge she said, "I am supposed to ask for the gift?"

The concierge smiled and replied with excitement, "You must be the lucky birthday girl!"

The Concierge gave Maya the key to her suite and the next hint.

The concierge then said, "Take this private elevator to your suite." Amazed, Maya took the envelop with the next clue from the concierge. Then she picked up her box with her new dress and shoes and stepped into the elevator. The concierge took out a key, turned the lock and the penthouse light came on. Maya stepped into the elevator and the doors closed. As she was riding in the elevator, she started thinking about the time and effort that Justin had put into this special day. When the elevator doors opened, Maya was mesmerized by the beauty of her suite. As she stepped onto the black marble tiled floor, the floor then transitioned into a plush black carpet. The suite was everything that she imagined her dream suite would be.

Maya set her box down and opened the envelope with the next clue. The clue read, "I hope you enjoy the suite. But the suite is not as sweet as the woman who will occupy it for the night. Your next clue is, get some rest...Grace Jones said it best in her most famous song. At 6:00PM it will be waiting for you."

Maya thought for a moment and said to herself, "Pull up to my bumper baby, in your long black limousine!" Then Maya exclaimed out loud, "WHAT!" Right then she sent Justin three thumbs up emojis. Maya walked around the suite, marveling at everything that was in it. She stepped into the bedroom and all she wanted to do was lay across the large memory foam king sized bed. Within minutes, Maya was fast asleep. At 5:30PM, the telephone rang.

"Hello!" Maya answered.

The voice on the other end said, "Wake up sleepy head, time to get up and get dressed...your destiny awaits." Then the phone went blank.

"Hello...Hello!" Maya yelled. Maya looked at the clock and seeing the time, she got out of bed and changed into her beautiful dress. It fit her perfectly and the shoes matched also. When the clock read 5:55 PM, Maya got on to the elevator and went down to the lobby. As she got to the first floor and the doors opened, there waiting was a black Phantom Rolls Royce limousine. Stunned, Maya walked over to the limo.

The doorman walked over to the door of the limo, smiled at Maya, opened the door and said, "You are looking lovely this evening...watch your step."

Maya got into the back of the limo and there set another clue. Maya opened the letter and it read,

"I want you to dine and ride on a wave tonight...tell that to the driver."

Puzzled, Maya pushed the intercom button and said, "I want to dine and ride on a wave tonight..."

The driver responded, "No problem Madame."

The driver began driving and took Maya to a secluded pier. The driver stopped and parked. Just then a blast of fireworks went off, and in the fireworks read, "Happy Birthday Maya!" After that a forty-foot yacht pulled up to the pier. Standing on the deck wearing a black tuxedo was Justin holding one single black rose. Maya just stared as the yacht docked.

Then Justin yelled out, "All aboard!" The walkway lowered.

Maya smiled and walked onto the yacht. Once Maya got on broad, she put both of her thumbs up into the air.

Justin smiled and then said, "So, how was your day?"

Maya walked over to Justin and didn't say a word. She put her arms around Justin's shoulders and neck and gave him a big hug. Then a tear rolled down her cheek.

As Maya pulled away from the embrace. Justin saw the tear and asked, "What's wrong?"

Maya looked at Justin and said, "Today was everything that I could have wanted in a birthday." Then she looked into Justin's eyes and kissed him on the cheek

. Justin smiled and said, "Did I miss anything?"

Maya thought for a second, smiled and said, "Well, you could have had me a male stripper..." and laughed.

Justin replied, "I will be your private dancer tonight..."

Maya stepped back looked Justin over and commented, "Oh really?!"

Justin then remarked, "Today, your wish is my command...within reason." And laughed again.

Maya thought for a second and then said, "A glass of champagne would be nice."

Just then, Justin produced two champagne flutes with Champagne filled about three-forth full. Justin handed Maya a glass and said, "A toast to the birthday girl!"

Maya touched glasses with Justin and replied, "CHEERS!"

They both took sips of the champagne and just then the yacht began to pull away from the dock.

Then Maya asked, "So where are we going now?"

Justin answered, "We are going on a fantastic voyage...so let's have a seat, enjoy the ride on the waves because dinner will be served shortly."

Maya sat down on the big plush chair and looked over the landscape as the yacht cruised along. Maya stared out and without moving her gaze she asked, "How did you do all of this?"

Justin smiled and answered, "It was a labor of love."

"How long have you been planning this?" Maya continued questioning but now looking at Justin.

Justin smiled and said, "Everything that you have gotten today, you have deserved. I am just glad that I could help make it happen."

Maya looked at Justin and saw him in a way that she had never seen him before. He was everything that she wanted in her dream man.

Then Justin asked, "So what did you like most about your day?"

Maya thought for a few seconds and said, "Out of everything, right now is what I liked most about today... Spending this time in this dress, in these shoes, on this yacht with my friend that made it all happen is the best part of today."

"Maya, is there anything that could have made it better?" Justin asked.

Maya stood up from her chair walked over to Justin and gave him one of the most passionate kisses he had ever had. As they kissed, Justin put his arms round Maya's waist. Maya put her arms round Justin's waist, and they continued their lip lock.

Then Justin broke the kiss and asked Maya, "What are we doing?"

Maya responded, "Kissing!" and let out a giggle.

Justin giggled also and said, "We are the best of friends, I don't want to Jeopardize that."

Maya paused and then said, "Real talk, how do you feel about me?
" Justin looked at Maya and remarked, "You can't tell?"

Maya looked at Justin, then she looked at her dress and shoes, then she looked over the landscape where they were cruising over and said, "How long have you felt this way?"

Justin replied, "I don't know. It kind of crept up on me." And began laughing. Then Justin asked Maya, "Well, how do you feel about me?"

Maya thought for a little while and replied, "To be honest, up until now, I saw you as my best friend." Then Maya paused. Justin looked at Maya and then looked over the watery landscape view and asked, "And now?"

Maya replied, "I see you as a whole lot more." Then she put her arms around Justin's waist again and asked, "Can I have another birthday kiss? I was really enjoying the first one."

Justin smiled and said, "Your wish is my command." And they enjoyed this kiss, the cruise and whatever else that the night and the future had to offer.

ELEVEN

ONE LOVE TRUE LOVE

*J*erry and Tracy had been married for 30 years. They had raised a family together and through all of the trials and tribulations of life, they were still happily together.

Jerry was set to retire within the next few weeks even though he had been eligible to retire for years. Tracy was a stay at home wife and mother throughout their marriage. It had been ten years since she felt like a real mother because all of the children had moved out or went away to college.

On this particular day Jerry came in from work. He was in a stoic mood. Tracy noticed his facial expression when Jerry walked through the front door.

"Hey sweetie, how was your day?" She walked over and kissed him on the cheek.

Jerry replied, "It was ok, but so many things in life have changed. As we are getting older, it is either someone is sick or someone has died."

"Baby, what happened?" Tracy inquired.

"Ross Green was diagnosed with prostate cancer yesterday and last week Garrett Jones died of a heart attack. I just keep thinking about us."

"What about us?" Tracy asked.

"I can't let a day go by without letting you know how much I love you. When I have to go on those company trips and you can't go, I feel like a part of me dies inside. Even after all of these years, a day doesn't go by that I don't feel like I was meant to be with you forever."

Shocked, Tracy said, "Sweetheart, every day for the past 30 years, as soon as you would leave for work, my heart would ache for you and I missed you every minute you were away."

Jerry looked at Tracy and smiled.

"That is so good to hear. Hey let's go out to dinner tonight?"

Tracy answered, "Sure! It has been a while since we have had a date night."

"Okay, go get all dolled up and I will hop into the shower and we will make a night of it."

Tracy smiled and kissed Jerry on the lips and said, "You are a good man. I love you."

Jerry smiled back at Tracy and responded, "You are a beautiful woman and a great wife and mother."

Tracy blushed and graciously accepted the compliment saying, "Well thank you my love!" Then she turned and walked into the bedroom.

Jerry followed behind Tracy and went into the closet. He pulled out his black suit and laid it across the bed. Then he went into the bathroom. Tracy put on a nice dress that had a designer print with a floral pattern. She sat at her cosmetic desk and looked into the mirror. As she began putting on her makeup, she thought about the different times in the past that her and Jerry shared and the memories brought a smile to her face. Then Tracy said to herself, "You know you are in love when every time you think of that person, a smile comes to your face." And she looked back towards the bedroom door.

Just then Jerry opened the bathroom door and walked out. Jerry noticed Tracy looking in his direction smiling.

"Tracy? What are you up to?" "Nothing baby, just thinking of you."

Jerry smiled and said, "Yeah Right!" And began laughing.

Tracy laughed and said, "I'm serious!" Jerry walked over to Tracy and placed his hands onto Tracy's shoulders and said, "That is a beautiful woman in that mirror."

Tracy touched Jerry's right hand and then stood up. Jerry placed his arms around Tracy's waist and Tracy placed her arms over Jerry's shoulders and around his neck. Then without any hesitation they began to kiss passionately. The kiss was if it was their first date so many years ago.

After a few seconds, Jerry broke the kiss and said, "You are trying to get something started up in here!"

Tracy smiled and said, "Yes I am!" Then she unzipped her dress and it fell to the floor. Jerry saw the lacey pink undergarments that Tracy was wearing and noticed how well they still fit her.

Then Jerry remarked, "That exercise class that you are taking is working its magic...damn you are fine!"

Tracy reached over and kissed Jerry on the cheek and looked into his eyes and said, "I do it for you."

Jerry kissed Tracy on the neck and on her earlobe and then he moved his suit onto the dresser and laid Tracy on the bed as if they were newlyweds again. As he kissed and caressed her body, he thought about their lives together.

He kissed all down Tracy's stomach and then kissed around the top of her breast. Then with his free hand he unlatched her bra.

Tracy whispered, "You still know how to unhook a bra one handed!"

Jerry replied, "Some skill, you never lose." Then he hungrily sucked Tracy's full bosom. Tracy held her hand on Jerry's head and just continued to let him have his way with her breast.

Jerry rolled over and Tracy began kissing Jerry's chest and then she kissed down to his stomach and took his testicles into her hand. She gently squeezed them. As she squeezed, Jerry became more and more aroused. Then Tracy began to kiss the tip of his manhood. Jerry looked down at Tracy and smiled. Tracy kissed, licked and sucked it for a few more seconds and then with her free hand, she took off her panties.

At that point, she climbed on top of Jerry and began riding him like a horse. The two of them got into an almost perfect rhythm. As Tracy moved to and fro, she got wetter and wetter. Jerry pawed Tracy's breast and licked her harden nipples one at a time going back and forth. Right then they picked up the rhythmic pace and just then in unison they said, "I'm cumming!"

Just then as they looked at each other, a strange feeling came over them and both of them grabbed their chests. They grabbed each other and held each other close. As they held each other, their heart rhythms began to beat as one and then the beat went slower and slower until their heart beats stopped.

Tracy's medical alert alarm went off and within minutes the paramedics were at the scene. When the paramedics opened the door, they found Tracy and Jerry embraced in each other's arms with smiles on their faces.

The paramedics checked for pulses and there were none for either of them. One paramedic said, "It looks like they came and went at the same time! I hope I am that lucky when it is my time to go!"

TWELVE

THREESOME

Nina was a sexy thick female. She was also very adventurous. She enjoyed the thrill of a challenge. Nina worked for a child welfare agency and enjoyed helping children.

One day while at work, her and a co-worker, Travis were having a conversation and that conversation turned into a topic of an intimate nature. Nina and Travis were friends with benefits. They would hook up from time to time.

While in this intimate conversation Travis asked Nina, "What is your sexual fantasy?"

Nina thought for a second and said, "I want to be with two guys at the same time."

Stunned, Travis replied, "Are you serious?!"

"YEP! I have always wanted to have that kind of sexual experience."

Travis thought for a second. "If you want Nina, I can hook that up for you."

Nina gave a big grin and said, "Who is the other person?"

Travis thought for a second and replied, "My brother Reggie! He is down for kinky shit like this. Hold on let me call him." Travis pulled out his phone and began dialing.

Nina, seeing that Travis was putting this fantasy together said, "Hold up, I said it was a fantasy...you seem a little too anxious." And she started laughing.

"Well either you want it or you don't!" Travis remarked. At that point, Reggie answered the phone.

"Hello.." "What's up Bruh?

I've got a live one!" "Man!

What are you talking about now?

" "Hold on."

Then Travis turned to Nina and said, "If you want this to happen it can."

And Travis handed Nina the phone. Nina looked at Travis and took the phone.

"Hello!" Reggie called out.

Nervously Nina responded, "Hey!" Then Reggie asked, "What is my brother up to?"

Nina laughed and said, "He says he can make my fantasy come true."

Intrigued, Reggie asked the question, "What is your fantasy?"

Nina blushed and then said, "I want a threesome..."

Reggie got quiet and then said, "Is this April Fool's Day or something?!

My brother is trying to play a joke on me!"

"No joke...we were at work talking about fantasies and that was mine."

"Yall, don't have work to do?" and Reggie began laughing.

"Yeah, we are gonna get back to work, but Travis made the call..."

Then Travis took the phone from Nina and said, "So are you down or what?"

"How does she look?"

"She is Straight!"

Reggie thought for a second, then asked, "She got a big booty?"

Travis started laughing and said, "Its fat!"

Nina asked, "What are you two talking about?"

Then Reggie said, "Yeah man, I'm in."

"Ok, this weekend..."

Then Travis looked at Nina. Nina smiled and shook her head in the affirmative.

"Ok then, Saturday night!" said Travis.

Then Reggie said, "Well, I have to get back to work and I am quite sure you two have to do the same."

Travis responded, "Ok bruh, talk to you later."

"Peace!" and they disconnected the call.

"So Nina, you are going to have your fantasy fulfilled."

Nina sat quietly for a few seconds and then asked "Travis, how does your brother look?"

"He is straight!"

"That's not telling me anything."

"Look, I don't judge dudes...but he gets his fair share of dates."

"Do you have a picture of him?"

"Yeah, hold on." Travis pulled out his cell phone and went into his gallery app.

Travis scrolled the photos and then said, "Here he is."

Nina looked at the photo and yelled, "Damn! He is cute!"

"So are you sure you are up for this Nina?"

Nina reclined back in her chair and said, "The question is, are you and your boy up for this? I know I can take it."

Travis chuckled and said, "Alright, we will see."

Nina looked at Travis and said, "I need to get back to work, but I am looking forward to this weekend."

"So am I..." Travis replied as he was leaving out of Nina's office.

As the weekend approached, Nina started thinking about what was going to happen. She thought, "Can I handle two men? What is expected of me? Will it hurt? Two men at the same time may be fun."

The big day finally arrived and Nina called Travis.

"Hello!" Travis answered.

"Hey Travis, this is Nina."

"Hey girl, what are you up too?"

"I am getting ready for tonight."

"So am I. My brother is geeked up for tonight too!"

"Travis, I can't wait! By the way, where are we meeting at?"

"You can come to my place at about 7:00pm."

"Ok, I will see you two at 7:00pm sharp and you all better be prepared."

Travis thought for a second and replied, "You are talking about condoms right?!"

"That too!" Nina responded.

"It's gonna be all good."

"Ok, see you tonight."

"See Ya." And Nina hung up the phone.

The evening came and Nina arrived at 7:00 PM sharp. She was dressed in a red satin dress and a pair of red six inch Stilettos. As she walked up to the door, she began to feel a little apprehensive. She pushed the door bell and waited. About 10 seconds went by and then the door opened. Both Travis and Reggie were standing at the door.

"Hello gorgeous!" the brother said as Nina walked through the door.

"Hi guys..." Nina responded.

"Well come on in and make yourself comfortable." Travis said. As Nina walked past the brothers, they could not take their eyes off of how the dress fit her body.

Reggie whispered to Travis, "Damn man! She is fine!"

Travis smiled and whispered back, "I told you she was straight!"

Then Nina turned around and said, "You must be Reggie..."

Reggie replied, "Were you expecting someone else?" and smiled.

Travis stepped in, "Let us go upstairs and all get better acquainted." They all proceeded upstairs and went into the living room. In the living room, there were three empty lead crystal champagne flutes and a bottle of Moet chilling in a chrome ice bucket.

Travis walked over and took the Champagne bottle out of the bucket and opened it. "POP!" The champagne erupted and shot out of the bottle. Then it subsided and ran down the side of the bottle. Reggie handed Travis a flute.

Travis poured the first glass and said, "Ladies first."

Nina took the glass of champagne and said, "Thank you very much."

Travis poured the next two glasses for he and his brother.

Reggie took his glass from Travis and said, "A toast to a night that we won't forget." Everyone followed with, "Cheers!"

As they all drank their champagne, Reggie asked Nina, "So where are all your friends? I know a fine woman like you has some friends."

Nina took a sip of the champagne and replied, "I don't have a lot of female friends and the ones that I do have aren't down for things like this."

Then Travis cut in, "So what are you down for?"

Nina took another sip of her champagne and said, "I am down for ANYTHING!"

Reggie reiterated, "ANYTHING!?"

Nina smiled with a devilish grin and said, "ANYTHING!" and then winked at both of the brothers.

At that point, Travis said, "Alright now, well let's get this party started and head to the bedroom!" All three of them took a big gulp of the last bit of Champagne that was in their glasses and proceed to the bedroom.

As they all walked down the hallway, Travis pointed to a door at the very end of the corridor. Nina walked up to the door but did not open it. Reggie walked up and opened the door.

When Nina looked into the room all she saw was a larger white room with no windows and a big black bed with a sheer black canopy vail all around it. As she walked into the room and walked towards the bed, she had unzipped her dress and it fell to the floor. All she was wearing was a black lace bra with matching panties, silk black stockings with garter belts and the six inch red Stilettos.

Nina looked back at the brothers and said seductively, "Whew, it's getting hot in here!"

Travis responded, "It's going to get much hotter!"

Reggie gave a grin and began unbuttoning his shirt. Nina jumped onto the bed and noticed that Travis had not taken anything off.

Nina questioned, "Are you scared?"

Travis responded, "Not at all!" But he still did not take any clothes off.

Reggie then said, "He will join in when the fun begins."

Nina smiled and rubbed her hand across Reggie's chest. "I can tell you stay in the gym!"

Reggie smiled confidently and said, "I spend my fair share of time there."

At that point, Reggie took off his pants and Nina saw the bulge in his underwear and rubbed the bulge.

While Nina rubbed the bulge, all she could say was, "Damn you are big!" Reggie just smiled, but didn't say anything else. Reggie reached over and grabbed Nina's right breast and hungrily began sucking it like a newborn baby.

Nina caressed Reggie's head and held it against her breast. Then Nina said, "That's it...suck that titty!" Nina reclined back onto the bed. Reggie took his free hand and rubbed all over Nina's body. Then his hand found its way between Nina's legs and he fondled her love canal until she was sloppy wet.

Then Reggie yelled out, "Niagara!"

Nina began laughing. Travis just stood and watched. Reggie began kissing down Nina's stomach and his head went between her legs. Reggie began kissing and licking Nina's clitoris.

Nina screamed out, "Hell yeah!" As Reggie worked his tongue in and out of the luscious wet flesh, Nina squirmed and then gyrated her hips back and forth. The gyrations became more rhythmic as Reggie licked and tongued all over Nina's womanliness. Then Reggie lifted Nina's legs and flickered his tongue on her perineum.

Nina yelled, "Oh shit...that's it!" As soon as Nina shout out, Reggie stuck half an inch of tongue in her asshole.

Nina squirmed and moved all over the bed not knowing how to react. Then she yelled, "I'm cumming!" at that very moment a gush of liquid squirted all over. Seeing this Travis walked over to the bed and unzipped his pants. Nina looked down at Travis and grabbed his crotch. Travis took off his pants and Nina without saying anything took his manhood into her mouth. She tongued the head and ran her tongue ring all over the shaft. Then she took in inch after inch until she felt a gagging sensation.

Travis changed position and said, "Now what?" Nina stopped her oral pleasuring of Travis and announced, "I want a dick in each hole!"

Shocked, Reggie sarcastically said, "We will need a third guy for one in each hole."

Then Reggie remarked, "Actually, you would need five more guys for every hole."

Nina began to laugh and said, "One in my pussy and one in my ass!

"Travis smiled and said, "So, you want that DP treatment?!"

Nina smiled and remarked, "I have always wanted to have two men. Maybe now, I can finally get some satisfaction!"

The two brothers looked at each other, then looked at Nina and said, "Your wish is our command!"

Reggie got on the bed and Nina climbed on top of Reggie. As she guided his penis into her vagina, she had a gush of wetness. As she rocked back and forth, Travis mounted Nina from behind and pulled her ass cheeks apart. Then with one quick thrust, Travis was riding on the Hersey highway.

"Oh shit! Goddamn you muthafucker you! I see I need two muthafucker to satisfy me!" Nina yelled with delight.

As the three became more rhythmic, juices flowed all over the bed. Within minutes, all at once, the threesome let out an orgasmic symphony. After what seemed like forever, all motion stopped, and everyone rolled over to a spot on the bed to recuperate.

As the silence began to become deafening, Nina exclaimed. "That was amazing!"

Reggie laid quietly in his section of the bed. Then all of a sudden Travis and Nina heard a loud noise coming from Reggie's direction. As they looked towards Reggie, they realized Reggie was snoring.

Travis half whispering said, "Damn girl! You put my brother to sleep!"

Nina smiled and said, "A girls got skills!"

Travis smiled and responded, "Skills to pay the bills!" and they both laughed. Then they looked at each other one last time before they both closed their eyes and fell into a deep coma like sleep. They began dreaming of the next time that they would all get together again for another love session.

From the Senses to Sensuality

From the Senses to Sensuality

ABOUT THE AUTHOR

SIKEMAN is one of Chicago's most dynamic open-mic poets. SIKEMAN's poetry is intense, passionate, profound, and thought provoking. SIKEMAN's poems touch on issues particular to the black community but are relevant to all of society.

While earning a BA degree from the prestigious University of Alabama, he also enhanced his ability to formulate his own type of poetry. SIKEMAN has been writing poetry for a number of years. In his poems, numerous issues are pondered in a search for the truth and the absolute

In his life he has endured countless numbers of trials and tribulations, heartaches and pains, downfalls and pitfalls, yet he courageously and continuously keeps striving for greater heights.

SIKEMAN is well known on the poetry scene for his graphic poem "Wounded Heart" which expresses the agony of love lost in a failed relationship. Another often requested poem *"You Know Me"* depicts Death in a humanistic form. The poem takes you on a trek with The Grim Reaper as he touches the lives of ancient to modern mankind and how he will continue to affect man until the end of time

.

From the Senses to Sensuality

 SIKEMAN's award winning poem "*Questions*", examines the true aspects of this journey man calls Life.

SIKEMAN has competed in and won many poetry competitions in the Chicagoland area and abroad. Past endeavors include having completed and self-published a book of poetry titled, "*Messages from Wild, Wild Hundreds*"

SIKEMAN also self-published the novella, T-Rex, A story from the hood. SIKEMAN has hosted numerous open-mic events for the up and coming record company, On Point Records. His most recent venture displays his artistic capabilities in the culinary realm having established wine tasting and food pairing events titled, From the Senses to Sensuality which inspired the book of short stories with the same title.

www.ingramcontent.com/pod-product-compliance
Lightning Source LLC
Chambersburg PA
CBHW022156240626
47153CB00007B/2691